The
Tale of
Riverhaven

Sienna Rapaport

Fresh Ink
an imprint of
SOCIETY OF YOUNG INKLINGS

Requests for information should be addressed to:
Society of Young Inklings, PO Box 26914, San Jose, CA 95126.

Cover Illustration: Kristen Schwartz

Interior Design and Composition: Beth Spencewood

Printed in the USA

First Printing: April 2023

ISBN: 978-1-956380-36-1

PART 1

Chapter I
The Vast Imagination of Melanie McGee

Melanie McGee was having the time of her life.

Squinting at the harsh sunlight, her thoughts drifted to how ordinary this town she was in looked, yet is so magical when you peer closer. Because, the thing is, that the town which Melanie is in is the exact opposite of ordinary. Why? Well, to start it off, because Melanie could feel proud to say that the miniature dragon at her side, nuzzling her shoulder, had not dared to take a step away from her. She grimaced at the thought of leaving all the grown unicorns alone, who were in fact, not that grown at all. They were quite a foolish species, she had to admit. No matter their age, they always seemed to find trouble. Leaving them unguarded surely meant the ghastly motion of being fired. Melanie McGee, who is no older than 12-years-old, was given the preposterous job of watching over the irritating mythical animals of the Riverhaven Zoo. The job was impossible. That, at least, was what nearly all the townsfolk had said.

The mysterious town of Riverhaven is truly like no other. It's filled to the brim (if that's even possible) with all types of unusual species. You never know if you might bump into some strange creature on the street. Unicorns, Dragons, Hippacles, Griffins, Monerines; the list could go on forever. The people of Riverhaven had disliked the creatures since the beginning of time. All they had ever wanted was to be left in peace. No foolish Unicorns, playful Griffins, repulsive Monerines (it is believed that their species is a cross between a goat and a sheep) or engrossing Hippacles to stop them.

Ever since the end of the Battle of The Diddod, the people of Riverhaven were never to live a regular life again. You see, the Battle of the Diddod was the worst in centuries, a war between possibly deadly creatures believed to be myths, ancient and powerful beings made straight from the earth... and the townsfolk. The people of Riverhaven already had to endure being stuck somewhere in the corner of the universe where no one had ever ventured. Having to be caged there with creatures that seemed to, in their perspective, go out of their way to irritate them, was eventually going to start a war. And so they did. The Unicorns had their magical horns, the Hippacles had their rock-solid skin to protect themselves, and the townsfolk had whatever weapon they could find in their homes. When the people of Riverhaven announced war against all of the odd creatures, the creatures were given the name: The Diddod. The townsfolk had decided upon this unusual name, considering that they thought of the creatures as repulsive and a threat. (For some peculiar reason, they had decided that "Didodd" had suited those personalities perfectly. Perhaps it was because "Didodd" is a word that rolled off of their tongues strangely. Or maybe it is because of the way they think "Didodd" sounded weird to them and they believed that should be the name of their enemy. Or perhaps they came upon that name by accident. I don't know the real truth. You can choose which definition sounds suitable.)

The war went on for 200 years; 200 long, bloody years. In the end, "The Didodd" won. They were allowed to stay in the town. No one could stop them. The people could declare more war, but no one wanted to relive the horrors of having no food, water, shelter...you get my point. But the most important thing about Riverhaven is the town, similar to the creatures residing in it, is believed to be a myth. Something— or should I say, someone—had made sure of that. But that is a story for another day. Melanie McGee is not an inhabitant of this town. But this is her story. And it is my job to tell it. So, I am going to take you to a place a lot nicer than the town of Riverhaven, and a lot more famous. I will be taking you to The Big Apple, La Manzana Grande, La Grosse Pomme ... New York (!)... where Melanie was born.

"New York is not a place for an imaginative child. It is not a place for a girl who likes to run, climb, dance and prance around the city like a baby. New York is for success. For attentive children. For children who follow the rules. For children that aren't foolish and aren't babies. You, my child, are not ready for New York."

This was the exact wording of Mr. McGee, Melanie's father, after Melanie had, once again, broken her arm, trying to catch a butterfly. It had been flying so elegantly, she remembered. It had landed on her nose with a light flutter. A shiver of delight had scurried through her skin, pulsing and throbbing in thrill. She had trailed behind it as it flew by bustling citizens, as it headed for the streets, headed for the cars, until... at last, it halted with a sudden motion. Melanie was a cheetah at that point. She couldn't stop. Her body flung itself onto the road, landing onto the firm cement with a crash. Cars screeched to a stop. Pain had flared up her arm but she tried to focus on the feeling of the cold cement. A man with curly brown hair up to his shoulders walked out of his car and carefully picked up Melanie's prostate body, making sure to not touch her bruised arm. She had been driven to the hospital immediately and was now pacing in her room, arm wrapped securely in a cast. "You're lucky to be alive," scowled her father, frowning deeply and shaking his head with worry.

These types of incidents were more of a ritual to Melanie. It happens at least once every three months. And if she was feeling particularly foolish, maybe even twice. Well, it may not always be breaking a bone of hers. Once she fell into a huge sewer hole and couldn't climb out, the other time, she thought she had seen a giant bunny and had run into a giant bush of poison ivy, leaving its mark for two full weeks. And every time she did so, her father's frown would dig deeper into his face and he would repeat the same words sternly. Then, he would give Melanie one last glare and leave her to think in silence. She knew that she was disappointing him, being a great business man and respected for his cleverness. Melanie would try to prevent her silliness, honestly... but it wasn't much use. To make matters worse, her father seemed to find the idea of having an imagination a disgrace.

Mr. McGee was the type of person who could instantly become popular within a matter of seconds among other adults. He was well known in the city of New York for his mathematical ability and his way with science. He has his own talk show where he discusses everything about the world and "exposes" things that are not true. He has an entire segment about how fake Riverhaven is, which makes him one the many who constantly claim that Riverhaven and the myths inside of it were no real place. Not that many people disagreed. Mr. McGee, however, has his quirks: He, even to his own daughter, doesn't really use his name often. Something about being embarrassed of it or some family thing. Melanie doesn't care. I bet that she sometimes wondered what he put on medical or government forms. If his name was anything like Sir Biffy Toad Moocoddle Trilee McGee, that would be my greatest laugh of the year. He is always leaving town unexpectedly and when he comes back, he doesn't mention any details of what happened, let alone tell Melanie where he goes. He has never, according to Melanie, written with pen and paper. Even when in a hurry, he would always use a typewriter. The, however, weirdest feature about him was that he kept a large, metal feather in his pocket. He prized it so much that it was always in his pockets. Does he bring it in the shower? I don't know. There was no way that the feather was created by a sculptor. Melanie was sure of it. Not even the best of the best could match the amount of detail woven into the metal. She was also sure that it was definitely not from any animal that she had heard of.

Melanie sometimes doubted if she actually was related to her father. He was clipped and formal while she was messy and adventurous. She wasn't a city girl, Melanie would tell herself. I am meant to be roaming rural landscapes, searching for hidden treasure and mythological creatures that my father says don't exist, I was just born this way. Or, she'd think on a bad day, maybe I'm just wrong, maybe books are books and I need to go and actually start my life. But Melanie knew better. She had read books about the Battle of Diddod. She couldn't help it, she was fascinated. Devouring book after book of fairy tales and myths had made her as curious as ever. But the way her father sternly scolded her for believing it just increased her curiosity.

And, that evening, the craziest thing happened. Her father promptly walked into her small creamy white bedroom and sat on the messy bed covered with flowers, scraps of paper, and enough junk to make her father wince and scoot away. He straightened, fixing his slightly dirty tuxedo from his day at work. He looked uncomfortable, so Melanie tried to pretend nothing was weird and smiled really brightly. Finally, he cleared his throat. "Melanie, I have come to realize that you aren't fit for this lifestyle."

Melanie rolled her eyes in an exaggerated fashion. She had heard those words many times. Her father has sent her to various parts of the world, bringing her to various boarding schools. She had never survived more than a week before she had been kicked out. No matter where she was sent to, she would always return, brighter and more inquisitive than ever. To me, I imagine it as being a frog being bumped to little lilapds each time the water ripples. To Mr. McGee, it's irritating and slightly embarrassing when the press found out. "You'll be going to Riverhaven," he continued blankly.

Melanie looked at him and started to laugh, thinking her dad was finally pulling an April Fools joke. His light blue eyes blinked back at her and Melanie's laughter ceased. Her eyes widened. He was serious.

"But... but..." she stuttered, "Um, I think you're not feeling well or something."

Now, don't get me wrong, this is what Melanie had always wanted. But she had always imagined herself convincing her father to explore the woods that everyone hated and play around. She had imagined stumbling across the town, her father's mouth dropping open and a sorry for everything he had said coming out of his mouth, she would smile and forgive him and walk into the town hand in hand and then... happily ever after I guess. Mr. McGee dully telling her she was going there didn't seem right.

She knew that the place existed somewhere but could never figure out where. And then her father comes along saying he does. Well, he didn't say that, thought Melanie. But if he was telling the truth... Her fake cheerfulness attitude was replaced with real joy and her dark empty insides fizzled with bright colorful hope. It died out as soon as she remembered who she was speaking to, the man who taunted anyone who believed in the town. "But father, you told me that place didn't exist. Do you actually believe in Riverhaven?

You found it? How? So you believe me now? Why did you go searching for it? Wait, did you go searching for it?" said Melanie quickly and excitedly but still doubtful.

Even If you didn't know Mr. McGee, you would never have to second guess what he was going to say. Of course he did not believe in the foolish land of Riverhaven. So, when Mr. McGee didn't laugh or narrow his eyes, he caught Melanie off guard. "Yes, Melanie, you will go to Riverhaven."

Melanie jumped up and down giddily, all the suspicion draining out of her."Really? You mean it? Thank you so much," she said, while running off to pack her bags. She didn't ask anything more.

The first shock that came to Melanie was the transportation. She had assumed that she was going to have to take an airplane or maybe even get to ride on a mythical creature from her books. Instead, her father ushered her into his musty, black limo-like car and let her watch from the window as they sped through roads for three full, uneventful hours. The second shock came when she arrived. Her father had pulled up to a dirt road that had appeared in where they were parked. Melanie didn't have to exaggerate when she said they were in the middle of nowhere. The car had driven through a thicket of woods that her father had called The Trenside Thicket. She faintly recalled that was the woods that he had forbidden her to go to the other day, however, her mind had been so clouded with emotions the memory slipped away. They had then driven on the highway by themselves, not a trace of a car in sight, though calling it the highway would be a stretch. The "road" was so bumpy at first that it had two etched lines that formed a pathway. Every time they moved, the tires hit something.

They had ultimately arrived at a long spiky gate that looked sharp enough to cut off Melanie's finger when touched. Mr. McGee explained that no one crossed through the forest since they were afraid of what was inside. He even wanted to get out of the forest as soon as he could. Slowly and deliberately, Mr. McGee creaked the spiked gate open, revealing a gurgle of gaping people and a couple of misshapen creatures that looked a lot like myths in her storybook, staring right at them like a human was the weirdest thing they had seen in decades.

Chapter 2
Riverhaven

After Melanie had entered the gates, grinning like she had won the lottery, Mr. McGee had sped off into the forest, wishing her luck in her new town. She walked up to the townsfolk when the gates had closed and tried to make friends. Everyone stood there silently and eyed her like they found it impossible that they had seen someone else of their own species. Once the shock had settled into their minds, they introduced Melanie to the creatures. Melanie noticed that one of the lady's tones had switched from welcoming to a cold bitterness when she looked at the large mud-colored animal that the lady called a Griffin. Melanie nodded at it approvingly, smiled at a Hippacle, gagged at the Monerine, and ran up to hug some Unicorns. For a moment, Melanie felt like she belonged...until she saw the townsfolk's faces. The truth dawned on her. How could she have forgotten? The war... She was probably the first in centuries to be happy to see all the nonsensical creatures. After Melanie apologized to the townsfolk and gave the creatures a look that said *don't worry, I still like you guys*, she started exploring the rest of the town, searching for a place she could stay. There was a small playground that looked unused. There were many sooty but cozy houses and a couple of rickety buildings, one of them a school. Melanie wondered what it would be like to learn there when the summer was over.

When Melanie passed a stunning white marble statue of a Unicorn, she smiled. Then she peered closer and saw that someone had gouged out the creature's eyes and replaced it with what looked like rotting food. Melanie turned and walked away, convincing herself not to cry and trying to find something that hadn't been murderously destroyed by the townsfolk. Upon finding a building with a dusty and rickety sign, labeled *Riverhaven Zoo: Come see some Myths!* Melanie walked in, entering a dark and kind of spooky corridor.

The door had been open but didn't feel like a welcome at all. It creaked and each step on the floorboards was like old bones cracking. The hallway smelled like dust. A cone of light came from a small window on the side which revealed a small table with a spider crawling up it. Before she could even take a couple more steps, a short, stubby nosed man with a couple strands of hair sticking out of his head, ran into her, his belly jiggling when he collided into her skinny, slender body. Melanie toppled backwards, knocking down a metal trophy laying on the dusty counter. The man looked at her in surprise, turned on the lights and shook his head, revealing to Melanie the color of his hair: the purest white, as if snow had decided to live on his head. He smiled, and a treadmill of some unnatural feeling twisted inside Melanie's body. His smile cocked to the side, showing a line of neat, white teeth. So white, that it might have been mistaken for his hair by some folks. A sea of wrinkles were painted onto his tanned skin with his arms, however, looking younger, as if they were aging at a slower pace than his head and hair.

"I haven't seen you around before," he simpered, peering at Melanie like he was trying to find a sign of her being a robot or hologram. "Besides myself, there hasn't been anyone new in town for decades."

Melanie smiled politely and let him continue. "Have you come to see the animals? I'm afraid that I was just closing for today..." he said. "But I can make an exception for a nice young fella. I have one myself, I know what they're like."

He winked and Melanie suddenly felt very unsteady, urging her legs to run. But stubbornness, one of her best traits, kept her going. "I'd like to see the animals," Melanie declared, deciding that she had nothing better to do and that no one in this town could be that dangerous, especially not a zookeeper.

"Well then, follow me. Oh," he added, "you can call me Mr. Bandswith."

"It's nice to meet you Mr. Bandswith," replied Melanie,

"I'm Melanie."

And just like that, the new girl in town made a sort-of new friend who she was only a fraction afraid of. But all the adults that you first meet start with an awkward relationship. And before she knew it, Mr. Bandswith uncovered her love for the mythical animals and let her live in his spare house in exchange for helping out in the zoo. Melanie loved her job. Not many people came to the zoo though, claiming that they had already seen enough of the creatures. Melanie would frown and continue her work, waiting for the moment where the anger boiling in her stomach would fade away. It never did.

Chapter 3
The Quest

"No one in the town appreciates you guys. Am I right, Sapphire?" said Melanie solemnly.

Sapphire is a Unicorn. I know it is a rare name for a Unicorn but I'm just happy it isn't Sprinkles or Rainbow, or worse... Doug. Moving on: While Melanie cleaned the unicorn pen the night before, she had found one of the unicorns sprawled on the floor, a small gash in its left hoof. Melanie had cleaned it up and they had instantly become friends, or at least as much of friends you can be when all the Unicorn can do is purr and neigh and nuzzle. After begging Mr. Bandswith over and over again, he reluctantly let Sapphire the Unicorn live with Melanie instead of in her pen. Melanie felt that it would be impolite if she hadn't given the creature she saved a name. "Sapphire," she had said, "Your name is Sapphire." The unicorn had neighed in approval and Melanie continued her work.

She supposed giving the unicorn a name was foolish. An act for a silly little girl with an imagination a little too vast. But not giving the unicorn a name didn't feel right. Melanie liked animals. And animals liked her. But they were starting to get on her nerves. Sapphire was fine... but the others in the zoo were becoming irritating. She felt pained to say it but she was starting to agree with the townsfolk. The animals were playful and fun. When she, however, came to Riverhaven, her hair was still light brown. Now it was a disheveled mess, caked with so much mud that she could have passed as a Griffin herself! Her once alert posture is now a sagging mess of skin and bone. Her wide and attentive eyes were now dim and circled with black exhaustion. Ever since she entered the town, she had known that the creatures and humans still held grudges. All she wanted right now was for her father to come back in his musty, black car and use his serious and strict attitude to straighten everyone up. But he wasn't here right now, and by the end of the summer, Melanie would be going to school in Riverhaven and live full time in Riverhaven; who knows how she'll be happy like this if the townsfolk are still mad at the animals. If she were to survive this place and stay here, she was going to have to change their behavior. Melanie sat down to collect her thoughts. She was not capable of keeping her excitement from a butterfly, more or less the excitement of helping a town so legendary that no one in the world felt capable of trying. So what could a 12 year old girl do? And what would she even do to help the animals and townsfolk? Therapy lessons?

Melanie was sitting in her office, which had been kindly given to her by Mr. Bandswith. She had already spent hours in there, answering angry letters from the townsfolk about shutting down the zoo, but now used the opportunity to search for some clue that would tell her how to stop the menacing war between the Didodd and the townsfolk. (Why in the world would she believe all of her answers would be here? Maybe it was because of how old and secretive the place looked? I don't know, I'm telling the story, not living it.)

All she needed to do was figure out what that *thing* was. A small door in the side of the room caught Melanie's eye. She reached for the doorknob and a thick, greasy, soot colored layer of what seems to be dust layered her palm. "Ugh, Gross!" she exclaimed, wiping down her hands on her dress. Using the smallest amount of finger possible she opened up the door and peered inside. She was standing in a spacious closet that smelled like humid air after it rains and little children's shoes after playing in the mud. A large pile of dusty cardboard boxes were stacked up in the corner, the flaps all open. She spilled out the contents of the boxes and the weirdest assortment of things fell out. A large, faded grey backpack with millions of pockets plopped out of the box first. Only later would Melanie realize the backpack was filled with water, food (way past the expiration date), a coat, extra pairs of clothes, a sleeping bag, five tins of purple cotton candy, and a diploma for graduating the best rated insect repellent creating university in Riverhaven (how many of those universities could there be?). Along with the backpack, out came a shiny, metal sword and a case, rope, the coolest silver armor, polished and cleaned so well it looked immaculate; and a pair of smooth brown boots with little springs at the bottom. Wow, all of these gadgets are so cool, thought Melanie. But this seems like materials for a quest, not the beginning of one.

Well… Melanie thought, If there is a bunch of questing materials in Mr. Bandswith's building, then he probably has an idea about ideas to help Riverhaven.

With a squeal, she dashed out of the room, Sapphire trotting beside her, and knocked on Mr. Bandswith's door.

"Mr. Bandswith, may I talk to you?"

"Ah, of course Malerie. Come in," replied Mr. Bandswith from the other side of the door.

Melanie groaned. In her head, she repeated, the same words she had done millions of times before: My name is Melanie. *Me-la-nie.* **Not** Malerie. (This was another thing I forgot to mention. Mr. Bandswith had a small issue with remembering names.)

But of course, she never said it out loud. If she had learned one thing from her father, it was to be polite.

"Mr. Bandswith, I am here to talk to you about saving the town," began Melanie, seated in a cushion-y armchair and facing her boss.

Mr. Bandswith chuckled. It was a bizarre thing to say.

Melanie looked down at Mr. Bandswith's hand which was fidgeting with a small shiny object in his pocket. He must be nervous that I'm confronting him, she thought, or quitting.

"Uh, don't worry I don't want to quit, you don't need to be nervous, I'm not quitting," she said, glancing back at his now unfidgiting hand. Mr. Bandswith smiled sheepishly but also in a way that said: never mention that again. Melanie cleared her throat.

"Um, I would like to make peace between us humans and the Diddod. Well, you are a townsfolk and you run a zoo so I was just thinking that maybe you'd have thought about finding a way to create harmony..."

Mr. Bandswith gave Melanie a long, sad look.

"Why don't you sit down, Melarie." He gestured to a large, cushioned arm chair and took a sip of his cup of tea.

"Now this is really something you shouldn't be meddling with."

"But I really want to. I need to. If I want to go to school here and live here, it can't be during some sort of cold war."

"Alright. Well, Magnolia, let me tell you a small story of

when I moved here last year."

Melanie could feel the insides of her stomach shifting back and forth. Why the suspense? It's freaking her out.

"I didn't even have to buy this zoo; it was abandoned and I just moved in. All the animals in the back were wounded and out of shape. I went around and cleaned them all and got them bandaged, cleaned the back and started setting up this small petting zoo. But there were scraps of metal everywhere and metal boxes so I went to clean them all out and this fell out."

He slid open a drawer in his desk and pulled out a long, ancient scroll, frayed at the edges and painted with a thin layer of dust. Mr. Bandswith handed it to her and she heartily opened it with a majestic gesture, showing a detailed treasure map. Sapphire jumped up, as if to say let me see. Melanie kneeled down to Sapphire's height and showed her the scroll.

"It's a map," she said, "That leads to some part in the Trenside Thicket. What is this?"

Melanie squinted at the handwriting. No one writes like that, she thought. No one. The writing was impossible to read. It was squished together like millions of sardines all trying to fit in one can. She had also noticed that the letter had been written with a quill, like it had been, either, made ages ago or someone who really preferred quills over pens.

Maybe that was Riverhaven's motto. Melanie discarded the thought, slapping her forehead angrily.

"Stay focused, Melanie and STOP worrying about unnecessary things."

Mr. Bandswith intervened.

"The scroll says to find: The Bird of Steel. The bird who controls the pathway between all the worlds. It says you must follow this certain path, and then, you will find him."

Melanie was silent for a moment until Mr. Bandswith said:

"I looked at it for a long time and if you look at the back of the scroll," Melanie tipped the scroll over to reveal more scribbled handwriting, "It explains that one singular feather from the bird of steel's back is a weapon to make anything you'd like come true. It holds the power to whoever is holding it to change anything they'd like. If we just find him and get one of his feathers, everything will work."

Melanie's spirits rose higher than the clouds, like a rocketship propelling itself up towards space. This quest will be so easy.

"I will come with you, Melanie," he said, sounding dignified and a tad bit dramatic, flashing a quick smile in Melanie's direction. She grinned, a large toothy one that took up her whole face. She hasn't smiled like that in forever. "Now give me the scroll. I will write down some notes," continued Mr. Bandswith, turning serious and speaking flatly.

Melanie shrugged, a little taken aback, and handed him the scroll. With a flourish, Mr. Bandswith snatched the scroll, obviously trying to be playful, but instead nearly ripping it in two.

"Sir, be careful," Melanie exclaimed.

Mr. Bandswith nodded distractedly, picking up a long, fragile quill and scribbling down some notes hastily. "Let's go Margaret. If we want to find the Bird of Steel," prodded Mr. Bandswith.

"Wait," replied Melanie anxiously, still gritting her teeth from being called otherwise, "I need to call my father. He must know that I am on a quest."

"That will not be necessary."

"Like I said, Magnolia, there will be no need to contact your father. I have it all under control. He doesn't need to know about this meager, little adventure. It will only take about a day. It'll be our own secret. What do you say we get some ice cream before we go," said Mr. Bandswith, winking.

She gave him one last look and then walked off, snatching her backpack, armor and sword as she turned around behind her and said:

"Let's go. We want to find this bird-man and get home

before sundown."

Little did she know that it would take much longer than that.

Chapter 4
King Henry and The Monerines

It had been days since Melanie had set off on her so-called "quest." But even she wasn't that patient. Her hair was a tangle of cobwebs, her face was covered in so much grime it took an effort to breathe normally, her shoes didn't seem like shoes anymore. They resembled a brown circle, all the salmon pink paint peeled off and a lot of brown gloop piled on it, which looked like some sort of animals food. And, with barely any doubt, Melanie was pretty sure that it was. She looked away in disgust.

"Have you found anything sir?" mumbled Melanie grumpily.

Like the millions of times before, Mr. Bandswith replied:

"No. Nothing."

Here Melanie was, hands dug deep in thick mud, in the middle of some endless forest, searching for... well, what? She was in search of some bird made of steel. Some bird who had such boundless knowledge and power, that it could grant Melanie's wish. Such a bird that she had decided to find because of a piece of paper. Should she really be doing this? And now that she was, what would such a bird be doing in the mud in a dry, earthy forest? Melanie sighed solemnly when she remembered how she began this journey. She had skipped into the forest, Mr. Bandswith trailing behind her, Sapphire galloping contentedly, a flower of hope blossoming in her chest. That hope had died long ago and she was starting to believe that she was never going to see the beloved Riverhaven again. In all the excitement, she had barely paid any attention to Sapphire who had been nudging her, pleading for food and some fresh water since the beginning of the trip. Melanie had none. She had eaten it all, sharing some with Sapphire and not even offering any to Mr. Bandswith at all. He was the one who got her into this mess anyway. He had, many times, led them in the completely opposite direction, claiming that the map had told them to go that way. He was wrong every time. He had also said that he saw a metal flash fly through the sky. There was no metal flash. He would apologize every time and crack a funny joke and flash the cocky smile of his but he would still be mistaken over and over again. At first, Melanie colored with shame. It was very unlike her to treat a person in such a manner. Father would not have been proud. But when she saw Mr. Bandswith's disapproving scowl, she thought that he could probably survive fine.

By the time they had started digging through mud, all the happy thoughts of saving the town had left her, leaving her as a ball of anger and grumpiness. Melanie peered at the tattered scroll again.

"Come on, guys. We're going this way."

Melanie pointed at a cluster of trees that she could've sworn they had passed minutes ago. But Melanie didn't mention it, not wanting her two companions to doubt her.

"I'm tired, Melanie," grumbled Mr. Bandswith, "Let's just go home and continue the search tomorrow. We can get a warm bath, some new, clean clothes, and some food."

A warm bath did sound nice, Melanie had to admit, and a new pair of clothes would be amazing right about now; but determination had already taken over. She gritted her teeth and strode into the cluster of trees, shouting behind her:

"Go home if you'd like to Mr. Bandswith but I am here to save the town."

The definition of friends was stretching between these two companions.

The more Melanie walked into the dim forest, the darker it seemed to get and the narrower the pathway between the trees became. The only light left was the flickering candle in Melanie's palm and the tiny glow of Sapphire's horn, which would illuminate when she was scared. A bush rustled behind them. Melanie spun around, clutching her candle like a weapon, since, in truth, it was her only one. She put her hand on Sapphire's silver fur to sooth her, but mostly to sooth herself. Mr. Bandswith was far behind, probably picking wild berries and devouring them like a dog. A sudden instinct to run propelled Melanie in the other direction, only to halt at the sight of two murky yellow eyes peering at her from the tree above. The woods was now pitch-black and Sapphire's horn was blazing like a fire.

"Mr. Bandswith," Melanie croaked, knowing that the angry zookeeper wouldn't be able to hear her, "It would be nice if you could come right around now." A second pair of eyes appeared, then a third, then a fourth. Swamp-yellow eyes were now appearing everywhere: behind Melanie, in which she whirled around—one hand clenched in fists, one right next to Sapphire, which made Melanie clutch her companion tight, and then millions of eyes encased the two in a tight circle.

Melanie prepared to scream. But then, a stout and pudgy man with greasy black hair and a muddy crown made of twigs and leaves appeared out of a bush.

"It's alright, my babies, these two... companions won't hurt you. I'll make sure of it," said the man to the millions of eyes.

Had that man seriously called those yellow-eyed

monsters his babies? He nodded in a weird sort of greeting to Melanie who stared back, not sure how to respond. She was still in the state of shock that I would call: I'm seriously considering if I'm still alive if I just saw a man who called those things BABIES!!! Then what everything the man said clicked.

"Us? Hurt... them?," Melanie retorted, forgetting about the best way to get out of these types of situations: being polite.

The man looked at Melanie in fake pity and fastened his crown as if to make a point that he was the king with the leaf crown. Super special.

"You little, foolish girl," he whispered dangerously, cocking his head to the side, "You think the woods belong to you, don't you?"

Melanie tried not to answer but it broke free anyway.

"Uh... No."

The man stepped closer. Melanie stepped back. How could she have forgotten what this woods was known for: danger, and very cuckoo people.

The man leaned into Melanie, his beady black eyes shining.

"But you are wrong, Melanie. This wood belongs to no one."

The man's breath smelled like rotting fish and dried seaweed, though there was no body of water in sight. Melanie gulped, not noticing how the man had known her name when she hadn't even told him it.

The man laughed but then hacked loudly, spitting dirty, fishy saliva into Melanie's face. She choked in disgust, wiping away the beads of fishy saliva from her face and suppressed the urge to run.

"I am King Henry!" the man declared.

Before she could stop herself, Melanie blurted:

"King of what? Dead fish?"

King Henry's blood boiled with rage and he raised his two pudgy fists to Melanie's face.

"I am King Henry!" he repeated, "Ruler of the East Woods," Melanie made a mental note that she was in the east, "Conqueror of The Devils, Master of Camouflage, and Protector of The Monarines."

Great, now she was facing a repulsive king with a reputation...

Melanie hadn't known how you could conquer devils or camouflage in the outfit the king wore, but the word "Monerine" did ring a bell.

At that instinct, Melanie understood what those eyes in the bushes were coming from. Millions of hulky, shriveled, brown animals walked out of their hiding, sharp teeth gnashed at the helpless travelers.

King Henry placed his dirty and grime-covered fingertip to Melanie's chin and whispered:

"I've wanted visitors for a long time."

Melanie felt sick to her stomach. She shivered, panic flaring through her like a police alarm. She could still smell the king's stale breath and could see the Monerines sauntering closer and closer to their leader. Sapphire whimpered, her horn's light casting eerie shadows in the trees. Melanie tried to sooth her by stroking the unicorn's fur but Melanie's fingertips were now quaking with fear. Mr. Bandswith was still nowhere in sight and Melanie, for the first time, regretted being stubborn. Melanie did the only thing she could think of, she chomped down on King Henry's muddy finger.

The king howled in pain, gripping the throbbing finger Melanie had just bitten. Melanie ran as fast as her legs could muster, screaming for no particular reason and spitting out the disgusting taste of uncleaned fingers. She glanced behind her to see Sapphire's path blocked by a Monerine, hunkering towards her in unsteady steps. Melanie's heart stopped.

"No!"

The Monerine... halted. A leafy vine was swinging

through the air, a dazzling and gorgeous, blond- haired girl with creamy white skin swooping down and grabbing Sapphire by the waist.

Melanie sighed in relief, forgetting about why a stranger had just appeared at the exact moment her companion was in danger. But then she saw that the ivy vine was swinging back into the tree where it had come from and the mysterious girl who had saved Sapphire had disappeared into the woods, bringing Melanie's only friend with her.

"N-N-No!" Melanie sobbed. "Where are you going? What are you doing?"

But the girl and Melanie's unicorn were gone.

Somewhere in the distance, King Henry roared:

"You will pay for this, Melanie! You'll see... One day you will regret what you've done!"

But Melanie wasn't paying attention. She sprinted away, eyes pricking with tears like a dam preventing the water to stream out.

Chapter 5
The Wizard

Melanie was still running, her messed up emotions pumping through her legs instead of blood. She replayed all the events of what happened in the forest over and over again, fighting back the tears welling up in her eyes and blurring her vision until Melanie had to stop running and had to wipe them. A random forest-girl had taken Sapphire, Mr. Bandswith was somewhere far behind her, and she was in a dark woods that could turn against her at any moment. She was alone and couldn't trust anyone.

The dirt path Melanie was walking on slowly turned into a field of grass. She was finally out of the forest! The sun was resting above the horizon and splashes of pink and orange spilled into each other like a watercolor painting. Endless fields of grass and flowers stretched out all the way to where the sun was resting. It was a beautiful sight. Melanie peered back up at the inky sky. The colors looked so fragile, almost like water. Thinking of water made Melanie's mouth dry out. She hadn't drunk or eaten anything in a day. Her satchel had no more food, just a blanket, some medicine, tin cans of purple cotton candy (she could eat that), her armor, Sapphire's brush to comb her fur and the map. A jolt of grief lurched in Melanie's heart. When all of this was over, she was going to find Sapphire and bring her back home. She promised herself.

The sun was now disappearing and the slightest hint of the moon appeared into the sky, obscured by clouds. It was time to go to bed. Pushing down the hunger in her stomach, Melanie dropped her backpack and took out her blanket. But there was something else hidden beneath the raggedy piece of cloth. A bright purple compass, streaked with stripes of ocean blue. Where did this come from? Had Mr. Bandswith put it in there? Surely he would have told her if he did. Melanie frowned in concentration. She stood up and walked around. Usually, a compass's arrow would've moved, but her compass stayed pointed in one direction: forward. This wasn't normal. The second peculiar feature of the compass was that there was a blood-red button on the side of it. Melanie considered pushing it but she knew that in the movies, whenever someone pressed a red button, nothing ever went well. So she ignored it. But of course, Melanie stepped forward in the direction that the compass was fixed on. She took a couple more steps. The arrow in the compass suddenly switched direction. Melanie squinted her eyes, fascinated. She turned left, and kept walking through the grass until a massive wooden cabin came into view. And when I mean massive, I mean the size of an apartment building. An apartment building made entirely of wood and painted blue. Melanie's heart fluttered in exhilaration. How many wonders she had seen in a week! A small stream snaked around the side of the building and Melanie exploded with elation. Before she could stop herself, she flung her bag to the side and raced toward the stream, submerging her head completely under the water and inhaling gulps after gulps of the river water. Melanie lifted her head out of the water and wiped her wet hair out of her face. She dove back down for more. She was starting to feel very groggy and disoriented and after every swallow of water, she felt more and more dizzy until her eyes were sagging and shutting down. She couldn't fall asleep now, not when she had gotten this far. The water must've been enchanted, she wailed silently. This must be a trap. Melanie knew sooner or later someone would try to stop her from finding the bird, however they knew. Melanie tried to stand up but her legs felt weaker than soft tendrils of vapor. Soft footsteps echoed behind her. Someone was coming. Melanie sprung to her feet, using all the energy left in her and… fainted into the arms of an old man who had appeared behind her.

"This must be her," a hushed, female voice whispered. Melanie's consciousness hovered between sleep and awake and felt herself gurgling and coughing out water.

"Shh..." soothed a deep, raspier voice, "sleep as long as you need, dear."

Melanie heaved in a breath and coughed again. Her throat felt dry, like the kind of feeling when you are so sick you don't notice it. Slowly, Melanie's eyelids unglued themselves from her skin and flickered open. Before her, stood a man with twice the amount of wrinkles as Mr. Bandswith with a very familiar face, ringlets of white hair and beard falling from his face and beard. He looked like a way, way younger version of Santa Claus. Melanie stared at him with wide eyes, shuddering as fear slashed through her face. No one should like Santa Claus who isn't Santa Claus. The man smiled serenely; he didn't look dangerous, just old and welcoming. His warm smile ignited in Melanie like a fire and she smiled back, weak but oddly relaxed.

"You're safe now, dear child," he pacified.

Melanie could feel her muscles relax as he spoke and lay limp and an outstretched bed.

He picked up a bowl filled with a shimmering golden liquid. A piece of white bread sat on a plate beside it.

Melanie's stomach, as if on cue, exploded into an orchestra of grumbles and screams for the food. Melanie tried to be suspicious of a gold-colored soup but her doubts caved into hunger and she ate it all in one swallow. Only after that did she remember the iconic parenting line of "never eat food from a stranger." Then why did this man feel familiar, just someone she's never met. The soup tasted like sugar and ripe fruit. Melanie licked her lips and reached out for more, only to see that there was none left. The man laughed. It sounded like a deep rumbling from the bottom of a lava pit, the warmth heartily rising up and bubbling over. It warmed Melanie to her toes.

"Um…" Melanie began, "Who are you?"

The old man smiled kindly. "Merlin, dear. My name is Merlin."

Melanie gazed at him, gobsmacked. "As in the Merlin of King Arthur? The Merlin in the fairy tales I read at home?" gushed Melanie.

He laughed again. "Why of course! Who else would I be?"

Melanie's insides did a flip. She wanted to hug him, ask for an autograph, touch him just to see if he was real.

"I see that you enjoyed my golden strackaberry soup," the man continued.

She goggled at him.

"Have you not heard of strackaberry?" he began, but then stopped, "Oh. How foolish of me. You aren't from here dear girl. What's your name?"

"Melanie," she answered, feeling unprofessional next to her role model, a man who spoke just like in the fairy tales; old, wise, and Shakespeare-ish.

She liked Merlin, though. Something in her could tell that he had already known her name all along.

"Melanie," he said, "I know that you're looking for the Bird of Steel."

Oddly, Melanie didn't feel a tiny bit surprised. She nodded and he continued.

"But this quest of yours is more than what it seems. Right now, anyone that tries to hurt you is your enemy. But soon, a greater one will arise and your goal is to vanquish that enemy."

Melanie shook her head, confused.

"Don't worry about it now," he added.

She slowly nodded, though not at all comprehending how you can be told that and just forget.

"Everyone has a special Bon—"

"Are you actually a wizard?" interrupted Melanie. She knew that she was being rude. She, however, was still stuck on the fact that a real life Merlin was standing in front of her, telling her about how special she was.

"Yes. Now, as I was saying, everyone has a special Bond with something. Bond in our world-yes, the Trenside Thicket is technically another world- is like a superpower of sorts. It may be a tiny bond. You may never learn what it is. But you, my dear, have a bond that I noticed the moment I set eyes on you," he said.

"And when was that?" asked Melanie.

"The day your father decided to send you to Riverhaven."

Melanie choked on air.

"B-Bu-But how?" she stuttered.

"I am a wizard, remember. I have been watching out for you along with a couple of friends."

Melanie furrowed her brow. "What friends?"

Merlin stepped to the side revealing a cluster of three girls and one boy. They all looked pretty normal except for one. Except for the one elegant and gorgeous blond-haired girl, creamy white hand stroking the fur of an uncomfortable looking silver unicorn that belonged to her.

"You!" Melanie gasped, charging at the girl, fists raised, ready to launch at her if she had to.

"Wait!" she squealed nervously, "Stop!"

Something in the girl's voice told Melanie that she meant to harm so she reluctantly halted.

"My name is Hazel," she began, "and these are Cora and Ashley."

Melanie smiled at Cora and Ashley, who both returned the favor, though one of their smiles was dripping with fake kindness. Hazel took a cautious step towards her.

"I didn't mean to take your unicorn. Cora and I have been watching you during your journey, master's orders." Melanie was about to ask who her master was, when Hazel, however, continued speaking.

"When I saw that the Monerine was going to attack, I panicked and brought your unicorn back here, knowing that you would eventually find the apartment."

Hazel glanced down at the compass in Melanie's pocket and smiled. Of course, Melanie thought, Merlin was leading me here. Then Hazel added, for good measure maybe:

"Could we... Maybe be friends?" she asked, probably expecting a no.

Melanie's inside lot up, but she didn't let it show. In truth, she had never really had a friend and she definitely wanted her first one to be a sweet unicorn-saving warrior.

"Of course!" Melanie squealed. And just like that, Melanie and Hazel were friends, officially.

Melanie's smile grew bigger as she looked at Cora who was smiling at the sweet moment.

"Hey Cora. Um... you seem nice," Melanie said lamely. Cora, obviously, found it not in the least lame at all. "Wanna be friends?"

Cora blushed. Melanie's heart was now throbbing with joy. In five minutes she had made two new friends. She never knew it would be so easy. Cora and Hazel. Cora and Hazel. Cora and Hazel.

Then, she remembered that there was a third girl. Ashley. Melanie turned to talk to the girl, excited, to only see she had been on her phone the whole time, typing furiously. Ashley's olive skin and sweeping red hair was nearly as beautiful as Hazel's features. But there was something different about her. Melanie realized what it was, disappointed. Ashley was scowling... at her.

"Oh Pa-Lea-seee. Don't be all sappy about friends. It's really not that big of a deal. Out of all the people in the woods," Ashley said, her voice bitter. "A *city girl* faces the destiny."

Melanie was first, hurt that Ashley had said something so horrible about the two girls, then jealous since it seemed Ashley had a lot of friends, and then about to ask her what she meant about destiny until Hazel stepped up in front of her defensively.

"Ashley!" she gasped, "Why would you say that? Melanie is kind, generous and loves the mythical creatures more than anything. I've been watching her for the past week! There is also a reason why the... um... thing chose her. Plus, being jealous isn't going to change it."

Melanie was definitely confused but was washed out by a feeling she had never felt before: belonging. Though I would still be slightly creeped out about two girls and an extremely old wizard spying on me. But Hazel had just... defended her. Melanie's face flushed a soft pink and a tiny smile played on her lips.

"Whatever," grumped Ashley, figuring that she had lost the battle of words. Then, she sashayed out of the room. The boy, who had been there moments ago was gone to.

Cora walked up to Melanie and said:

"Ashley is the winner of The Young Trenside Beauty Pageant so she thinks the woods belong to her."

Cora rolled her eyes and Melanie giggled.

"And she's very possessive. But sooner or later, you learn to like her a bit. She's not all that bad," chimed Hazel.

"That's the problem with Hazel, Melanie," teased Cora, grinning. "She always finds a way to like everyone."

Hazel pretended to look offended and then fell down laughing. Melanie's heart glowed.

"That's my Bond," said Hazel, "Trusting everyone and everything eventually. Sometimes that's a good thing and a bad thing."

"Mine is swordplay," said Cora.

Melanie inspected Cora's loose jeans and sweatshirt and the black, silky bob as her hair and could imagine her holding a sword perfectly.

"What's my Bond?" wondered Melanie out loud.

"I was about to tell you before you charged at dear Hazel," replied a profound voice behind her.

The three girls spun to find Merlin, sitting in a chair with a cup of tea, listening to their conversation. Melanie had completely forgotten that he was there.

"Oh, um... sorry, uh, sir... master... holly ... Uh wizard Merlin ma'am" she said, flushing a deep crimson.

"It's quite alright, but please" he added. "Call me Merlin. Now, as I was saying before, you have a special bond with mythical animals. You can hear their thoughts and wishes if you learn how to. There will be a time when you will need to join forces. When you make a real friendship with the animals, you'll be free. You will always make friends with them and, one day, they will help you battle in a war that's soon to come."

"A war!?" Melanie gasped, "I did not sign up for that. I'm just trying to find a bird. What does that have to do with a war? Was that what Ashley was talking about? When Hazel said there was a "thing" that had something to do with a destiny, did it have to do with this? Why is this so much bigger than a bird? Do you always talk like this?"

"When Hazel said destiny, dear, she was using the wrong term. Nobody knows your final destiny, you choose that and pave the road of your choosing. But there is an enemy you will fight in the near future. One that will start a war."

Melanie gaped at him, suddenly wanting to go home and feeling way too young for this. Wars never meant good things, it meant deaths and very sad endings. It meant a terrible fate for what is left of Riverhaven.

"Don't worry," said Hazel, placing a hand on her shoulder.

"We'll help you fight," added Cora.

Melanie smiled gratefully at her new friends but didn't feel relieved, remembering when Mr. Bandswith had said that this was just a meager adventure. That it would be over in a day.

Someone grumbled behind her. She turned to find a boy with slick black hair spiked up at the sides and extremely thin eyebrows, glaring at her. While she had been introduced to Ashley, Cora, and Hazel, Melanie had barely even glanced at him. He was the boy who disappeared when Ashley had gone.

"Melanie," said Merlin calmly, as if he knew he had to sugarcoat what was happening next to restrain me.

"This is Oliver," interrupted Hazel, her voice switching from supportive to fierce and unkind.

Melanie gave Hazel and Cora a *why-do-you-two-not-like-him* look. Cora shook her head.

"We'll tell you later," mouthed Hazel.

The boy slashed his piercing eyes towards Melanie, gritted his teeth, and stormed out of the room.

"What was that all about?" she asked.

"No time for explanations Melanie. We have something to discuss and then you'll be back on your way," said Merlin. "Cora, Hazel," Merlin gestured at the two to sit down.

Wow, that was fast.

"Melanie, when you learn your bond, it is your greatest ally. It will help you with everything. Remember that," he said. Then, like nothing had happened, he switched topics.

"I have a present for each of you girls."

Cora and Hazel glanced at Melanie in excitement, clasping their hands together and staring Merlin down eagerly. It's just a present, Melanie thought. But then, she saw what Merlin was doing. Strips of purple liquid were being pulled out of his chest, molding into various objects before it split into three bubbles of translucent purple water, hovering above each of the girl's head.

"Hazel," said Merlin, waving his hand side to side dramatically. The water above Hazel's head turned into a locket with a gold heart clinging from the chain, majestic and glowing in the purple light. It lowered into Hazel's hand, solid. The three girls gasped. "This locket will let you see into two people's hearts, literally. Put the golden heart above the person's heart and you will hear all of their thoughts and wishes. And if you really want to, you can grant one of them. You can grant anyone's. But beware, you can only use it twice." The present drifted to Hazel's lap, the purple glow still there. Hazel clutched the locket like the world depended on it.

"Cora," said Merlin, intertwining his hands and making a beautiful blue-speckled silver sword appear before Cora's head. Cora's body limped in a mix of surprise and uttermost happiness. "This sword is the most powerful sword in the word. Once belonging to King Arthur, now... to you. Excalibur."

Cora's mouth twisted and then she did something that I always said wasn't such a probable thing to do when someone gives you a sword. She fainted. As in full on falling out of consciousness with her tongue hanging to the side. (Ok, maybe I made up the mat part.) "And last but not least," chuckled Merlin, smiling slyly at Melanie who was now bursting with anticipation. "Melanie." The liquid above Melanie's head slowly morphed into a golden bracelet, carefully draping itself onto her wrist. She sagged in disappointment. A bracelet? Yes, Hazel had also gotten jewelry but it was way cooler than this, she thought. Merlin noticed her face and he began talking:

"This is no ordinary bracelet, Melanie. Remember, these presents have to do with your Bond. Made entirely of pure gold, this bracelet, if you tap it three times, something magical will come to the rescue. But, like many powerful magical elements, it can only be used once. You'll know when the time comes."

Melanie's sagging posture alerted and she gave Merlin a toothy grin.

"Now, you, Cora, Hazel, and Sapphire must go. You have a bird to find. But before you do, let me tell you this. This compass will always direct you to me. If you ever need me, the compass will show you the way. And, there's water in the kitchen. That'll wake up Cora."

And just like that, Merlin disappeared into thin air leaving his smoky blue trail to linger in the room and the three girls were left with a quest to finish.

Chapter 6
The Bird of Steel

Melanie and her three companions were back in the woods. When Cora had woken up, they'd gone back into the Trenside with new clothes and a full belly. While they began walking, they had ran into Mr. Bandswith who scolded Melanie for running off. Now, Hazel, Melanie, and Cora were chattering away, Sapphire behind them and a grumbling Mr. Bandswith ahead. When Mr. Bandswith had found them, he was so incredibly unhappy that she had other people coming he pulled Melanie to the side, his face red like a cooked tomato.

"Who are these girls Millie? Where'd you find them? This is the Trenside Thicket. You can't trust anyone."

Melanie decided to not tell Mr. Bandswith about her encounter with Merlin or anything that happened since they got separated. Instead she said, "I just bumped into them in the woods. They say they used to live in Riverhaven and would be happy to help. They won't be a problem at all." Mr. Bandswith hugged in an irritated fashion and kept walking. But the amount of times he turned to look at the girls made

Melanie wonder if he was the problem in this situation.

Melanie glanced down at the map and saw something she hadn't seen before. A landmark! With a... feather imprinted on the side. The Bird of Steel! Melanie squealed and everyone turned to her.

"We may have a chance to save the town after all."

Melanie had seen it on the map. The large, circular object that she assumed was a stage. This time, ignoring Mr. Bandswith's protests, she used the map and guided the three. With Sapphire trotting beside her, Mr. Bandswith unable to use the map and ruin their chance, and the warm air feeling fresh and welcoming, Melanie knew that luck was on her side and that she was going to fulfill her wish. But like how I always say it: Saying that you know something is a strong term, like saying you hate a certain person or saying that you've never done a certain thing. Melanie was taking quite a risk saying that she knew it was going to work. And maybe she's right. But I like to say that Melanie jinxed herself. That she had expectations that were a little too high, like how her imagination was just a little too vast. Because that night, when she arrived at the circular stage, where she was supposed to find the legend of the Bird of Steel, no one was there...

Melanie had ran forward pushing past bushes (that end up whacking Mr. Bandswith) and saw a clearing where a large wooden stage stood. She didn't even bother to check on Mr. Bandswith or the girls behind her. Because she was ready to see the Bird of Steel emerge. But after one awkward minute, Melanie's smile was limp. Have you ever been so sad or disappointed that your math just falls and your body feels so wearied that a random chill just walks up your spine? Well, that's what happened to Melanie. As if a needle had been injected in her, the numbness of her body was so overwhelming all she could feel was the slashing pain of her defect echoing the words: You failed. You failed.

"This. This can't be. W.We worked so hard, traveled so far... and the bird isn't here."

Melanie's heart went from the steady pace of a gazelle to the roars of a race car. This was her chance to prove to her strict, well-educated father and the whole New York that she was worthy, that she could be the mature young lady that her father had wanted her to be. She was ready to turn around, leaving her only chance of being worth it... until she saw Mr. Bandswith. He, like always, was fidgeting with something in his pocket. But this time, she could see the object. It was a long, detailed, metallic feather. A feather that Melanie recognized. A feather that her father always had with him.

"Mr. Bandswith?" said Melanie, bewildered, "Why do you have my fathers feather with you?" Melanie gaped at the smooth feather cradled in her father's arms. It was the one that her father simply adored. The one that he never let anyone touch. She was confused.

Mr. Bandswith smiled mischievously. Leisurely and not at all frightened, he pulled off all the hair on his head. But it wasn't hair at all. It was a wig. When taking it off, a patch of dark grey hair was revealed. Hazel gripped Melanie's arm, trying to sooth her. Melanie didn't feel it. Cora ran up to her father, sword raised but stopped when she saw Melanie's hurt and twisted face. They both knew they had to wait, they first needed some answers. Mr. Bandswith wasn't an odd and annoying man. He's Melabies father. And Melanie knows that he'd only dress up this way and constantly ruin her quest if he wanted something from her. Even if Melanie didn't like Mr. Bandswith, a sharp stab of betrayal hit her in the chest. What was going on?

"Melanie," he said, "I know I haven't told you much. My name is Walter Bandswith McGee. And yes, I am your father. I have much to tell you. So, I guess I'll start from the beginning," began Mr. McGee, not even waiting for his daughter's stuttered reply and acting like he was writing down a dull and emotionless autobiography about himself. "As a young boy, I had, much like you, a wild imagination and a longing to see the beloved city of Riverhaven. You see, Melanie, at the time, it wasn't unusual to believe in that town. In fact, it was quite the opposite. Many people had lived there, seen it with their own two eyes. Most people came back. They did not want to get entangled with the war between the Didodd and the townsfolk. I, however, was one of the few children who never got to see it. And it was for the same reason that I sent you away. I had an imagination a little too vast, much like yours. I was indeed quite popular among the New Yorkers. But that was only when it came to science and math. I would be popular, people would hang out with me, but if I found trouble, everyone would scamper away, until my foolishness had stopped.

"Over the years, I became less and less silly and more and more the lonely child longing to see a famous town. Yes, I had grown, but no one wanted to take any chances with me anymore. They left me friendless and alone, with nothing but a longing and a broken heart to motivate me. That was, until, one day, I completely disappeared. I ran away from my only home. I had to see the town. It wasn't the town itself that I longed for. It was The Bird of Steel. But more importantly, his power. I had read and heard that if you were to snatch one of the bird's metal feathers, you would receive all its power. The power could save the world... or destroy it. All I wanted was revenge. I would show the pesky children that I was no silly little boy anymore. I wanted them to see that they had made a big mistake," said Mr. McGee, bitterly. His lip curled slightly and he pressed them back together, though he wasn't looking at any one in particular.

Melanie's face twisted with stabs of emotion.

She hated her father for the lies he had created, the trouble he had made Melanie go through, the sinking feeling of defeat piercing her heart. She despised the idea of hurting a bird and a couple of kids. Why was it so necessary for her father to have revenge? It seemed like he needed an excuse for revenge, like he needed it to stay sane. Something clicked.

"R-Revenge," she gasped, little gasps coming out of her mouth afterward, "That's your Bond! That's-" She was about to say horrible. It is pretty horrible. Yet... he was still her father, wasn't he? He was still the man who had served her the warm, nurturing hot cocoa after she went to explore the frost woods draped in snow during the winter. He was still the father who had sung her to sleep when she was feeling restless. He was still the father who she had loved, despite his clipped attitude and issue with imagination.

"Why, dad? If they were bullies... if they began to ignore you, couldn't you have solved your resentment in a less... evil way?," whispered Melanie softly.

Like before, Mr. McGee stayed silent. There was still one more question nagging at Melanie's brain.

"If you had that power though, father—why didn't you stop the war? You could've made peace between the animals and the humans?

Walter dismissed the question with a wave of his hand. Melanie seethed, noticing that her father seemed to be uncomfortable with the question.

"Now, now, Melanie," said Walter. "Let me continue. When I arrived at Riverhaven, it was pure chaos. I had heard that humans and the Didodd were at war, but I never expected it to be so… gruesome, bloody, and cruel. I had nowhere to start. But then, one day, while I strolled through town, searching for a clue, a faint, hushed whisper spoke to me. That whisper told me to create a map and write down some exact amount of measurements and words which, after years since it happened, I don't remember. That is the mao you are holding right now. I kept trying to sabotage your trip but you just can't give up, can you. So I guess I need to keep explaining. Anyway, it said that, after doing so, I must follow the map and I would find the Bird. And I guess it'll be no surprise for you if I say that, after following the whisper's instructions, I found it. That whisper, I later concluded, must have been the bird itself. The difference, Melanie, between me and the bird was that the bird wasn't smart enough to realize that I was coming for his power. I had launched at the rascal and, before I knew it, had snatched the metal feather right off its back. I don't remember much, but I do remember the deafening crack that sounded right when I pulled it off.

When I gripped the feather, a scurry of power had pulsed through my eyes and mouth, pouring out of them in steaming heaps. I could feel the sizzles of the heat river down my spine. It was the most amazing feeling I had ever felt, Melanie. At that moment, nothing mattered. The war wasn't my concern, the children who ran away from me became foolish. The thing that I fidget with all the time is the feather itself. That is why I never told you my name. That is why I always use a typewriter. No one can know that I wrote that scroll. I left the town to make sure no one would go looking for me. In my head, I decided that no one could know I took the bird's power. Not even you, Melanie. I know your heart, and you would have handed me in to the authorities and then would have figured a way to clear my name but you still would do what's right."

"Of course I should do what's right," whispered Melanie aghast.

"But I solve my problems differently," said Walter, eyes fierce, "I motivate through revenge. No compromises or talking out of it. When I'm insulted... I will make sure that the person who insulted me would regret it. Once I had gained the power and ransacked the Bird's, I went back to New York. With success, I created my own news station, as you know— *The McGee Show: The Truth of the World*—convincing the majority of the world that Riverhaven wasn't real. I wanted no one to hear of my unlimited power. I didn't want anyone to steal it. There were a couple who still believed in the impish bird and Riverhaven. They would protest, yes. But they were soon to become known as insane and that they've lost their minds. And, words are powerful, Melanie. I ended up manipulating all of the people into a smart way of not believing their experiences at the town. Because the bird is no more, I hold the remainder of its power. I am The Bird of Steel."

Melanie's tornado of thoughts halted. Her heartbeat seemed to stop altogether. Silence. Silence.

Her father... The Bird of Steel? *Impossible.* She already knew, yes. But him saying it out loud made it ten times more real. And the feather of all that power was right before her, bathed majestically in the moonlight.

How was it possible, she thought, that out of all people, her nerdy, favored father was the one who had caused all the chaos? He could've stopped the war. He could've... well, solved all the worthwhile problems in the world. But he had used his power to punish scared and mistaken children who were now adults, probably married, with children ...if her father had let them live. Melanie tried to speak but her voice rattled in her throat. No. That wasn't her father. NO.

No.

No.

No No NO.

Her father was good. Her. Father. Was. Good. Right? Whatever he had done, it could still be fixed. She would not let this journey be in vain.

"Father..." she simpered, imagining herself boldly standing up to him, "Please hand me the feather. I know that there is still something in you that wants to stop this turmoil of chaos in Riverhaven. There must be a reason."

Walter shot her an irritated look.

"I was teased for my imagination. When I got that feather, Melanie, no one ever -E-VER- disrespected me again. Those children long forgotten, the town labeled as a myth, I became the pride of New York. I studied science, mathematics, and other worthwhile studies. If I saved Riverhaven, the townspeople would leave their town and venture to other cities, like ours. They would tell everyone where they were from and what the Diddod was like. I would become a joke. Everyone would trash my name for the lies I had told, Melanie," growled Walter.

Was this all, seriously, for a couple of teasing children? Was it worth it?

Melanie turned for Cora and Hazel but... they were gone. Melanie's panic rose higher. There was a piece of Hazel's pants flung onto the ground and a small silky black ribbon on the grass. No, not ribbon, hair, Cora's hair. The panic turned to breath stopping horror. Melanie couldn't think straight. What had happened? She couldn't do this without her friends. Were they in danger? Walter looked at her questioningly and Melanie flung away, concentration searing out her other thoughts before she could think up another panicking thought.

A silly idea, like all Melanie's other ones, popped into her head. If she wanted to save Riverhaven, she would have to attempt it. It was most likely the worst idea she had yet, but it was worth a try. She pretended to look unhappy (which she was, I guess. So, more unhappy than before,) and eyed her father carefully. She saw him rub his palms against the side of the metallic feather. She watched as he fidgeted uncertainly with the tip. She studied him as he lifted up the feather, pinched it with his fingers, and began twirling it endlessly among his fingertips. This was her chance. As fast as a human could possibly move, Melanie jumped up, rapidly yanked the metal feather right out of her father's fingers, and ran as fast as she could, into the vast woods that led to nowhere. She nearly stopped moving. The power that had just overflowed her body, kept her swaying and feeling like the weight of the world had been placed on her delicate shoulders, red dots dancing across her vision. Sweat filled her palms and Melanie remembered the feather she was trying to hold. The pain didn't subside but... she still felt amazing! Like she could do anything. Melanie was now suddenly running three times faster than before.

Less than two seconds later, she heard her father's angry footsteps right behind her heels. His hand swiped through the air, trying to wrench the feather out of Melanie's sweaty but firm hand.

As if Walter had just given up, he stopped his running and whistled loudly. The whole forest went silent. A bird chirped. The trees rustled. And then an explosion of sounds burst into the air. The first thing Melanie noticed was the smell of smoke, if she hadn't been overwhelmed by that, then she definitely was when a bloodthirsty dragon appeared beside her and roared, allowing the flaming fire in his mouth to escape and scatter all over the floor, not hitting Melanie but scorching Sapphire's tail. Sapphire yelped and Melanie rushed to extinguish the flame. The blazing inferno circled Melanie threateningly, smoldering a nearby tree and setting an unbearable amount of smoke in the air. Melanie coughed and swallowed many times, eyes watering with the sting of the smoke. She looked behind her. Fire. Fire. There was fire everywhere. Trees were now igniting faster than the speeding thump-thumps of Melanie's racing heart. There was only one tree, she could see, that stood still, though its branches were all twisted and weakening. Hands up in a surrender, Melanie screamed for help. She screamed for her dad, who also seemed to be screaming, somewhere behind all of the smoke layers. Sapphire's wings were now torched in flame and the poor unicorn crumpled to the ground, defeated and in pain. Melanie thought of all the times she had read books on brave princes and princesses slaying dragons, never imagining that she would eventually have to face one in the near future herself. A spark caught onto Melanie's thin-layered pants and she screeched, believing that she was about to die and crumble into flames, holding a feather that could cause all of that destruction.

"Did you really think I would come without protection?" Walter said somewhere in the background, but he sounded scared too.

Her father still loved her, he hadn't heard the flame catch onto her pants. Melanie knew her dad's mission: get the feather and Melanie will be safe. But Melanie wasn't safe. She was bathing in a flame that was going to kill her and Sapphire was already an unconscious lump on the floor.

Melanie wept, swatting cautiously at the flame creeping up her shirt that was now searing her arm and causing an explosion of blisters to erupt from her skin.

"Sapphire?" Melanie wailed hysterically.

Sapphire lifted her head and limped to her side in an instant.

"Can you fly?"

Sapphire raised her sweltering wing and winced in pain. There was some water and a lot of medicine creams in Melanie's satchel. The satchel, however, was still hanging on her back and even a second could be enough time to engulf her in flames completely. Melanie groaned and then began to weep again.

The satchel on Melanie's back fell and cracked open, revealing a bent and nearly broken twig that had somehow gotten stuck in there.

"Sapphire!" she cried, "I have an idea!"

It wasn't much of an idea but Melanie thought, she glanced up at the closest tree, the only one that wasn't burning to the ground and watched as one of the branches depleted— maybe she could climb the tree. She picked up a rock from the floor and threw it as hard as she could at the dragon's eye. For about 2 seconds, the dragon stopped roaring and blinked in confusion. When he saw that Melanie had reached the old, withered tree and was beginning to climb it, he bellowed out of his disorientation and spat another fireball towards Melanie's head, missing her by an inch but burning her hair slightly. Melanie yelped in astonishment. She may not have cared as much about her appearance as the other girls in the city, but she did like her hair quite a bit. She reached out her sweat-drenched hand

and tried to grip a part of the tree. There was nothing to hold on to. Below her, Sapphire yowled at her, urging her to move forward. Melanie yelped as another fireball grazed her nose. Screaming in pain as her legs dangerously dangled over the dragon's snapping mouth, she tried holding onto the branch with one hand and getting her bracelet with the other. If she could tap her bracelet three times. forget it. Melanie was holding on to the branch with one arm and just couldn't reach. Her hand slipped and she couldn't catch her fall and, before she knew it, she was plummeting towards a wall of fire, about to burn her to ashes. She screamed, knowing that this was her last moment on earth and that the feather in her pocket would fall into her fathers arms. At that moment, Melanie wished with all her strength for a savior. She wished for someone to free her from the torment of rage, bleakness, and turbulence creating the heavy storm in her heart. But most importantly. Melanie gripped her hands in a prayer. She wished for someone to save her from the field of flames that were about to swallow her whole.

No one came.

Melanie's grief was now too big for tears. She could hear her father crying out, like he didn't think his daughter could be so stupid that she was actually going to get set aflame. She wouldn't even live to be scolded for all this trouble.

She was going to die. She wasn't even going to get to hear her father apologize.

But just then, Melanie's miracle came true. Looking back at it, Melanie called it luck or a great strength, but I like to think that it was the bond of true friendship that had saved Melanie. Because it wasn't a warrior that saved her, it wasn't a miracle or a coincidence, it was a fire-consumed unicorn using all of its strength, maybe even her life, to save a friend that she had come to love during the long journey.

Chapter 7
Saved

When Melanie opened her eyes, she saw her savior looking at her nervously. Melanie smiled through choked tears of relief, sadness, and betrayal. Somewhere in the distance, there was a man with a grey patch of hair, extinguishing the wildfire he had made with buckets of water, howling in anguish. He had lost all his power.

Melanie felt oddly calm as she lay in the sky, watching the clouds drift away and New York City come closer and closer. That was, until, her balance in the air started wavering and she felt herself rising and falling in the air unsteadily. She looked up. Sapphire was looking ahead, a determined look on her face, despite her wings, blackened and shriveled. How could Melanie have forgotten? She was sitting in the air, reflecting on what had just happened, while her new companion was struggling to stay alive saving her. All the blended emotions tugging at Melanie's heart were flooded with guilt. Melanie tried to stand up but slipped and was now dangling from Sapphire's foot, so close to colliding with a building that Melanie would've fainted if she wasn't in such a dire situation. She screamed the capacity of a siren.

Melanie had left her satchel in the forest, which had probably burned to cinders and served as a good collection of pride to the dragon. In her satchel, she had kept all the medicine and survival equipment for if anything bad would've happened. All she had was a sword, armor, and cotton Candy. And even if she did have the bag, there was no way she could apply medicine to Sapphire in the air. At this point, Sapphire was failing to stay conscious under the burn of her feathers and the unbearable weight of a 12 year old girl. Melanie looked down at her dangling feet over the rooftops of the homes in New York City and could taste bile in her throat. Her palms grew slick with cold sweat. Melanie had taken pride in her fearlessness. No claustrophobia, arachnophobia, or … Fear of heights. But as she looked at the people walking on the sidewalk miles below and the way Sapphire looked like she was about to plunge down on top of them, a queasiness churned in her stomach like butter.

"I think I'm gonna throw up," she gaged. "I might as well just fall."

Melanie's grip loosened on Sapphire's foot as a sweat barrier covered her palms. Melanie gritted her teeth and forced herself to not look down. Sapphire's wide eyes were now slowly drooping and the two companions dived down another ten feet before Sapphire brought them back up. The last meal Melanie had eaten the night before was starting to crawl up her throat. She swallowed the putrid taste and attempted, and failed, to ease the roaring avalanche of nausea crashing down on her in waves. Before she could think about what she was doing, Melanie tore out a strip of her soot-covered pants and wrapped it around Sapphire's wing. Melanie let one of her hands break away from the hoof she was clinging to and wiped the pools of sweat onto her shirt. Then, she looked down again. That was her mistake. Because, if you've ever been clinging from a seared and nearly unconscious Unicorn hoof with one sweaty hand above the skyscrapers in New York City, (which I really do hope you haven't) you should never, ever look down. Melanie had looked down moments ago but that had been when Sapphire was close to touching the floor. They were now soaring in the sky, occasionally falling down a couple feet. Melanie let go of Sapphire in shock. As Melanie hurtled through the air, she could see Sapphire sigh in relief and steady her wings a bit better. Not completely, but better. Melanie knew that her weight added a million other problems to Sapphire's flight. At least one of the two of us will make it out alive, she thought, almost bitterly.

The bitterness left and was replaced with a mixture of hope and dread as she realized where she was propelling towards: The Hudson River. When Melanie hit the water, she could feel every bone in her body break at least a thousand times. It was strange, she would have died, unless Sapphire still had some magic left in her! But Melanie didn't even try to reach the surface. She just let herself drown deep into the river, not opening her eyes and knowing that she wouldn't be able to breathe. She would die, in an excruciating amount of pain... but saving a unicorn's life. That was, until, that same unicorn plunked deep into the waters beside her, sighing in relief as the water soaked into her charred wings. Then, Sapphire propped Melanie on her back and submerged out of the river, where a crowd of people—including Channel 4 News— stood, gaping.

Melanie's first thought was that she had to get to a hospital. The agony and ache of everything is literally unexplainable there isn't even a big enough word. Her next thought was that she should choke out the water in her lungs before it took over. Then she thought that Cora and Hazel were in trouble. She had to save them from whoever had kidnapped them. Her final thought was that she should probably address the news reporter who had jumped to her side, sticking a microphone in her face.

"We just saw you fall tens of hundreds of feet from the sky? How are you still alive? No offense, I mean, but... What is that? Is that a unicorn? Why does the unicorn have black wings? How can there be a unicorn? Is it dead? What happened to your clothes? Where did you come from? Are you Mr. McGee's daughter? You look a lot like him. What is your name? Where is Mr. McGee? Does he know about this? What happened? Are you an actress?" flurried the rather plump news reporter with excitement, urging the Channel 4 news camera to zoom into Melanie's probably bruised face and Sapphire who had emerged from the water and was glimmering in the sunlight, her wings normal but slightly bent.

Melanie nearly fell back with exhaustion. Every single bone in her body was screeching in the worst pain imaginable. Can you imagine it? If you have, then you are nowhere close. Double it by 200 and then come back to me. Melanie choked on her words. She was still marveling over the fact that she was alive and that a burnt unicorn had saved her. Melanie was motionless on the grass, trying to tilt her head towards Sapphire, even though she already knew that her faithful companion was sleeping. Melanie looked at the reporter who was hovering above her, asking her everything except if she was hurt. Guilt flushed into Melanie's cheeks when she thought about what she was about to do, because, for even if Melanie loved her father and still acted more foolish than any 2 year old, she had a pure heart of gold and wasn't going to let the poor town she had ventured to, suffer any longer. She took a long, shaking breath and spit out the whole story, beginning with getting the job at the zoo and ending with landing in the spot she was standing in right now. She stopped speaking and looked back. The whole crowd was standing there, ogling at her, speechless. Before anyone could utter another word, Melanie gurgled and fainted on the floor, laying there as she, along with Sapphire, were rushed to the hospital and restored back to health.

Chapter 8
Gone

It had been around a year since Melanie had traveled to Riverhaven. It felt more like decades. Sapphire had been cured from her little fire encounter first: The doctors had a hard time asking for the patient's name. Melanie had been saved afterwards, with no problems with neighing for an answer or an irritated and baffled doctor.

Her father was currently sitting in an empty cell in a mostly empty jail on the outskirts of the city. Melanie still missed him a lot and wished every day that she could've said something where Riverhaven had been saved and her dad turned back to normal. But that story is coming soon.

Melanie, who is now 13, doesn't have much of a home. Ever since she had been saved from Sapphire, they had become inseparable and the greatest of friends. She and Sapphire were currently on a world tour, surfing through countries, educating all of the families about Riverhaven and the terrifying moments they had experienced to save it. It was a lot of pressure, but Melanie knew it had to be done.

Starting from the week she arrived back in the city, Melanie had been on countless TV shows explaining the story of the beloved town and how it was now safe and full of heartwarming animals and people. Since Melanie had snatched the feather from her father, The Bird of Steel, it meant that she had inherited the power herself. Melanie felt threatened knowing that she could inherit all that and knew that many other people in the world would try to threaten her. So, she decided upon stopping the war among the Diddod and the townsfolk. Melanie had done this by murmuring a string of random letters that had popped into her head, though she didn't know how or why. The moment she finished, Melanie had scorched the feather in fire, hacked at it with whatever utensil she could find, flung it across the room, grilled it on the grill and baked in the oven. Yet it remained undamaged, not even a scratch etched into its metal coating. Eventually, she decided upon locking it in a massive safe that she only knew the code to and didn't mention its location in any of her interviews. She buried the safe deep below the fields of The Riverhaven Zoo, where, now free mythical creatures used to be caged. Melanie now resided in that town herself, living in a small house in a tinier cottage with a gentle woman named Natalie (and Sapphire) who had taken her in the moment Melanie entered Foster Care. The town of Riverhaven was now a welcoming town, full of tourists. Because of her. Melanie's life had turned from an ordinary girl's to someone who was usually on the news, or in an interview. (She had to admit, it was a bit overwhelming sometimes.) Or speaking to her father in jail, who had softened to her and had become more or less an amiable man.

"Melanie, my heart has sifted through revenge and hate for a long time... but is now in the right place... with you," Walter had said.

In three months he would get to leave the jail and come back to her. Melanie daydreamed of the time when she would truly get to see her father again. And when he was back, all of the adventures could begin.

You would probably assume that this is the end of the story, but you are wrong. Yes, it does sound like an ending, but something happened that changed the course of Melanie's life, and the lives of everyone else in the world. Around two months after the switch in Melanie's life, she was on a TV show in Australia, towards the end of her world tour and only a month away until her father left jail, repeating to everyone her story.

At that same moment, miles upon miles away in a jailhouse bordering New York City, a man with a dark grey patch of hair switched off the Australian TV Channel. He smiled wickedly.

"You've had your moment, Melanie dear, now it's time for mine."

Minutes later, a harassed and nervous looking man bustled into the Australian TV Show, panting as if he had run a long way. He bolted up to the interviewer and whispered something in her ear. The interviewer flushed a pale shade of white like a sheet of paper.

"Switch to the world channel," she stuttered in a quivering voice.

"Citizens of the world", the interviewer said, "we interrupt this interview with breaking news, the man known as Walter Bandswith McGee, has just escaped from prison and was last sighted heading in the direction of Riverhaven.

Part 2

82

Chapter 9
The Revenge of Walter McGee

Melanie McgGee was standing in an empty jail cell alongside multiple detectives and polices conversing in hushed tones. Many people would assume that Melanie herself was in jail, but those who thought that were incredibly wrong. Days ago, a man that the CNN news interviewer had called Walter Bandswith McGee had scampered through a hole in the wall of his cell (that took 2 months to make) and dashed off into the star-speckled night sky.

This hole was no accident. This hole was coated in purpose. Hot, burning tears trickled down Melanie's cheek as she surveyed the empty, grime-covered cell that her father had stood in just days ago. Melanie had visited her father a countless number of times when he was in jail, believing all of his words about his change of heart. She had taken in this same cell, even her disheveled father, and found nothing suspicious. Yet she never noticed the hole that Walter had probably taken months to chip in the wall.

Was this one of the other things that her father had tried to hide from her? How could he betray her like that?

Again?

Another rush of tears slithered out of Melanie's wide, emerald eyes. A police officer who looked large and muscled enough to snap a wrestler's neck in half without breaking a sweat, came over to Melanie and stroked her back, trying to sooth her. Melanie knew that most of the world by now wanted her in jail like her father had been, believing Melanie had somehow helped him with the escape. When Natalie, Melanie's foster mother had mournfully told this to her, she had recoiled back, aghast. The policeman, no doubt, probably agreed with the rest of the world, though, like how Natalie had soothed, he had no proof (for many reasons including that she had been on the other side of the world when it had happened.)

Melanie instantly stiffened and wiped her tears away. She thanked him for his assistance and scooted in a different direction, giving the empty cell one last loathing look.

"It's okay Melanie, dear. I'm sorry for what I have done. The feather's power blinded me. You were right about it. But you must understand, now I've changed. Melanie, my heart has sifted through revenge and hate for a long time... but is now in the right place... with you."

Melanie looked in her father's pleading face, and slowly nodded. Walter touched Melanie's wrist gently, fingers lightly caressing the space below her scrunchie, an accessory that helps tie up your hair. Tears were welling up in Melanie's eyes, but she fought them back. After weeks of asking, she finally believed him. But as she turned to go, she did not notice the gleam of triumph in her father's eyes.

That was the last time Melanie had heard from her father before he ran away. She had been stabbed with a knife of betrayal once, never imagining that, if it would happen again, it would be from her own father.

Her tears had turned from silent beads of sorrow to a mess of droplets and snot, sprayed over her face like one of Picasso's abstract paintings.

Her father had left.

Without apologizing.

Without explaining his choices.

Without even saying goodbye.

Melanie glanced down at her scrunchie, which had become quite a trend among girls her age, wistfully.

For this was no ordinary hair tie. Melanie, who was an exceptional sewer, had stitched the scrunchie open and had placed a paper with a string of numbers printed on it inside. 387724. This string of numbers opened the safe to the most dangerous object in the world. One that her father had in his possession for many, many years. Melanie herself didn't know the extent to those powers but they were nearly limitless, she knew. That object could most likely help Melanie find her father, right?

Could the metallic feather Melanie had tried everything to destroy help her?

There was only one way to figure out...

Melanie pushed past the policemen who were surveying the area and rushed out to breath the fresh, vanilla-smelling air.

She was going back to Riverhaven.

Chapter 10
The Vanishings

Melanie was never good at lying. When she ran away from home to "try to become a queen" when she was 7 and told everyone that she was in the backyard the whole time, no one believed her. When she accidentally got mud on her father's clothes and said that she had found them in her dresser like that, she was punished for ruining his stuff and for lying. So when Melanie told her foster mother, Natalie, that someone in Riverhaven wanted to interview her, Natalie saw right through her plan. Just not entirely.

"Melanie, If you're homesick, then you can just tell me."

Melanie had nodded distractedly, already coming up with ideas for how to track her dad. Could she call upon an animal to help her? Melanie looked down at the golden bracelet on her wrist. A very wise wizard named Merlin had given it to her, saying she would know when to use it when the time came. Was that time now? No, Melanie decided. I will find another way.

Melanie was now in Natalie's car, driving through The

Trenside Thicket, the woods that everyone feared and that Melanie had adventured through with Sapphire and her two friends Cora and Hazel. Thinking of her faithful companions made Melanie want to cry and cry until she ran out of tears. Ever since Melanie figured out who her father really was, Cora and Hazel had gone missing, the only clue of what happened still in Melanie's pocket, a strip of Hazel's pants, torn and on the ground when Melanie had found it. She had analyzed and analyzed the fabric from every angle. Nothing.

The car pulled up to a long spiky gate, the entrance to Riverhaven. Melanie's fears caved into the happiness of the town. It had once been a gloomy place, full of townspeople planning to rid off the animals trying to stay alive and away from the townspeople. Now, there were marble statues of people petting unicorns, plaques in honor of brave Riverhaven heroes and their animal companions, and so on. The fresh, humid air warmed Melanie's senses. Natalie opened up the door and she took in the atmosphere of her beloved town.

"I'll be at the house, Melanie," called Natalie.

"Alright," Melanie called back.

Melanie sauntered through the town hall, smiling, completely forgetting about the reason she was here in the first place. Something was wrong, Melanie suddenly realized. But what? A sensation of dread pooled into Melanie's skin but she couldn't identify why. The townsfolk looked pretty happy. The Griffins were playing on the streets. The Hippacles were swinging from fences happily. The Monerines were minding their own business. Melanie ran her hand through Sapphire's unicorn fur. Melanie jumped. Unicorns! There were no unicorns in the town, Melanie thought. Unicorns were always frolicking through the streets, or at least making a rainbow display somewhere. But none of the fuzzy, silver horned creatures were on site. Where had they gone? Melanie saw a woman with a crisp green coat walking nearby.

"Excuse me, ma'am," said Melanie, "Where have all the unicorns gone?"

The woman stopped short and gave her a dubious look.

"Are you new in town?" asked the woman in a high, shrill voice that sounded more like a mouse's than human, "because everyone knows where they've gone. What's your name?"

Melanie pondered what the lady said for a moment and answered:

"My name's Melanie... um McGee." Melanie knew pretty well that she was famous. Mentioning her last name to the woman would most likely arouse a bunch of smiles, hugs, and maybe even an autograph. But instead, the woman's face dawned with horror.

"M-Me-Melanie?!" she shrieked.

The entire town turned towards her, making Melanie flush a deep scarlet. At first, she thought that the woman was happy to see her. She had saved their town after all. But the lady's face was bleached white and everyone was staring at Melanie, petrified.

"Police!" the lady shouted, "Police! Police! We've found her."

Melanie glanced side to side, eyes narrowed in confusion.

"I'm sorry, what's happening?"

"Don't play innocent!" a man in the crowd shouted.

"Yeah!" roared another.

"You know perfectly well that you've been making all of the unicorns vanish," scowled a girl a couple feet away.

Making the unicorns vanish?

The crowd was now getting closer to her.

"You liar."

"You saved the town and know you're taking away our new friends!"

"What's that unicorn doing there? Are you gonna make her disappear too?"

Insults were now being thrown at Melanie like

cannonballs and hitting her cold in the chest.

"Unicorns... Unicorns are disappearing?" wheezed Melanie.

Sirens rang in the distance. The crowd inched closer, trapping her and shooting more ice cold rampages.

"We trusted you! We loved you!

"You're a menace, a shame to our town!"

"Riverhaven doesn't want you!"

Melanie's eyes glistened with tears. Riverhaven had been the only place that accepted her, that made her feel a little less like a caged animal. And now, she was being accused of something. But even worse, she was being accused of vanishing the *unicorns*. She adores unicorns.

"Bu-But I didn't do that," pleaded Melanie, voice rasping. "I swear."

The crowd was now feet away. A man lunged at her. Melanie yelped and shuffled to the side. A young boy clawed at her legs and a gash opened up, making Melanie cry out in pain and run to the other side. Police were now streaming out of their cars and pushing past the crowd, trying to get to Melanie. They thought she was a criminal and Melanie couldn't find a way to convince them that they were wrong.

"No," she rasped, "this is a mistake."

The crowd looked bloodthirsty now. The feeling of

deja vu reminded Melanie a lot of when she and Sapphire had faced a pack of hungry Monerines and a very scary man named King Henry last year. At the time, Melanie had been younger and more foolish. And instead of running, she had tried to bargain with the man who called himself King. But she was smarter now and wasn't going to make the same mistake. Melanie could only think of one thing to do. She lowered to her knees and dashed below the scuttling feet of the crowd, dashing into the Trenside Thicket, going everywhere but away from the realization that she was framed.

"Innocent people don't run!" roared a woman in the distance.

As Melanie ran, she thought of how wrong that lady was.

Chapter 11
The Foster Child

Natalie loved kids, especially the unique ones. So when Melanie McGee, a girl who had risked herself for a town that no one believed in, went into foster care, Natalie had come in to take her. Natalie knew how kind this girl was. Her imagination and thoughts were always so silly.

"One day, I'm going to make cupcakes fly."

"Dragon's will someday become henchmen to Hipaccles."

"I can camouflage just as well as a chameleon."

Her ideas always seemed so impossible, yet she had a heart of gold and loved the animals of Riverhaven. So imagine Natalie's surprise when she flicked on the TV and a clip of Melanie running from police showed up.

"Melanie McGee, a girl who is said to have saved the town is making our animals slowly disappear, starting with the unicorns," said a reporter.

"Unicorns?" murmured Natalie, "Melanie loves unicorns. She lives with one."

"Was it even Melanie who saved the town? The people suspect a new hero in the woods has come to light and Miss McGee just took the credit. Police are still investigating the traitor's whereabouts."

Natalie choked on her pasta. How could anyone come to that conclusion? She flicked off the TV. Her child was somewhere in the woods, police looking for her and surely lost. Natalie sprung to her feet and charged out the door. Melanie needed her.

Chapter 12
Lazorus the Troll

Melanie knew what it was like to go hungry. She had gone into the woods to find The Bird of Steel and had eaten all the food on the first day of the trip. A man named Merlin had saved her with a delicious stackaberry soup. Right now, that was all that Melanie wanted. Melanie hadn't had time to bring anything into the woods except for a tiny bag with a sword, some armor and a really strange diploma for a university that she had gotten last year. If I had known that police were going to track me, I would have come prepared, thought Melanie.

After she had run all the way into the middle of the forest, completely lost, she remembered that she had come to find her father. It was too late now. The safe was in Riverhaven and she couldn't go back there. Even if she wanted to. Melanie knew very well that there were some crazy leaders in the forest, some more scary than others. It was dangerous to be in the Trenside Thicket. Very dangerous. Behind her, Sapphire was panting like a hog, trying to keep up with Melanie's fast pace. A cry of pain echoed through the trees. Then another. Then another. Melanie halted, heart hammering. The screams were coming from animals. Mythical animals. Melanie charged towards the sounds. She wasn't paying the least amount of attention to the string that had caught beneath her feet. She only noticed when it was too late. Her foot snagged onto the rope and she propelled upwards, a net wrapped around her and Sapphire. The unicorn whimpered. Tiny -tiny- footsteps came from a couple yards away. Melanie slashed at the net. She kicked and punched but nothing happened. She grabbed her sword and flailed it around not knowing what she was doing. The footsteps were closer now. Melanie prepared to see a monster. Instead, a grime-covered troll who was maybe the size of a stuffed animal with a long spiky, grey beard and a red cone hat appeared out of the bushes. He grinded his teeth in excitement.

"You two will make an excellent addition to my army," he prowled, voice squeaky but taunting. He ran his hands through his hair, found a buff on it and then put it in his mouth. Melanie could've just died right there. Disgusting.

Yup, your typical bad guy in the Thicket.

Melanie thrashed at the binds on her wrists but it was no use.

"Aah," said the troll, amused. "You have a weapon, huh? I'll take that." He grabbed the sword, despite Melanie's grip on it and, with a surprising amount of strength, it heaved the net-covered companions to the floor and dragged them into an opening in the woods. A field of animals lay before Melanie. Griffins, Monarines, Hippacles, Dragons, misshapen animals, beautiful creatures; each of their eyes filled with sorrow. Melanie stared at them, her own eyes filling with tears. What had the troll done to them?

"My name's Lazorus," grumbled the troll in Melanie's direction. " 'Been keeping these animals here. No unicorns though, almost all of 'em seemed to have disappeared."

Melanie's breath caught and she peered at the creatures. Some of them had body parts that looked like they were slowly fading away. They're actually vanishing, thought Melanie. Someone is making the animals of Riverhaven disappear. And made me look responsible. Melanie swallowed.

"I've actually caught m'self a unicorn. You'll be a part of my special collection. Sit tight," said Lazorus, "I'm going to eat my lunch."

Lazorus left the opening in the forest.

"Help us," said a tiny whisper in Melanie's head. Melanie turned.

"Help us get out of here."

It was a Monerine... speaking to Melanie.

"You have a special bond with mythical animals. You

can hear their thoughts and wishes if you learn how to."

Merlin's voice echoed in her head. She was listening to a Monerine's thoughts. Melanie had always known the Monerines as bloodthirsty, unkind, and an animal that could never be hurt. But staring at the helpless creature, Melanie saw them differently. She had to free these animals.

Sapphire was whimpering loudly now, a piece of the net bound around her hoof. Cries and yowls scattered through the sea of hurt creatures.

"Animals of Riverhaven," Melanie began, "I've always thought that you could all fend for yourselves." Hushed animal whispers echoed in Melanie's head. "But I was wrong. We all need to be a team. We need to work together to get out of here. Animals, we need to mix our powers together. We will all get out of here together."

Creatures roared in approval and she saw that the Monerine's eyes weren't glistening with sorrow anymore... but with hope. Melanie may have just had her most amazing idea yet.

A rip silenced the crowd. The net that was holding Melanie and Sapphire was tearing apart, magically falling to the ground.

"There will be a time when you will need to join forces. When you make the real friendship with the animals, you'll be free."

At the time, Melanie didn't know what Merlin meant when he had said that. When she uncovered the truth of how the animals felt, she'd be free. How had Merlin known? When he said free, he literally meant free from the net. Melanie smiled.

"Oh, Merlin."

"Free us, master," whispered a Hippacle.

Melanie ran around, untying the rope around all the creatures. Before Melanie could command any further, Monarines were taking pieces of their skinned armor and morphing it with other powers from other animals. Dragons added a spark of fire onto Sapphire's horn, small enough so that she wouldn't get burned. Then, the plan commenced.

Chapter 13
The Escape

Lazorus was eating a lunch of pickled leafs and twig soup when he heard the spark of a fire. He rushed into the opening to find a unicorn with a glowing horn and a spark of fire igniting a tree.

"What are you doing?" he bellowed.

The girl named Melanie smiled at him apologetically The tree that had been ignited withered to ashes and all of the dragons he collected lined up in a circle on top of the ashes. Lazorus didn't know this but dragons could gain extra power when they stood on the remains of a fire. At least the dragons in Riverhaven could. The Hippacles and Monerines jumped onto the dragon's backs and shoulders, their forged armor gleaming in the sunlight. The dragons rose into the air and the rest of the creatures sprung up and pushed with their hands (claws, hooves, etc) allowing the dragons to rise higher. Then, Melanie launched herself forward, dragging Sapphire aboard and climbing up the chain of dragons into the sky. Then, they were gone, Lazorus gaping at the pile of ashes and loose ropes that they had left behind.

As Melanie soared into the sky, a warm sort of happiness wormed its way into her stomach. The wind breezed her hair and freedom felt like such an easy thing to get at that moment. The dragon's flying slowed down. Then she remembered her father, who had escaped from jail, lied to her and was somewhere in the world. What was she thinking? Going deeper into the woods when she needed to get that feather. But there was a whole town there. What was she supposed to do?

Melanie put her hands in her pocket and felt the squared compass that she had kept in there since she'd gotten it. The compass would always lead her to Merlin, a kind and incredibly smart wizard that she had befriended during her journey to get the Bird of Steel. The arrow was now pointing to the West. Merlin was the only person she could trust at the moment. Melanie was about to ask the dragons to fly right, when she, however, saw why she was flying so slowly. One of the dragon's wings was slowly fading away, turning stiff then soft, fading and then crumbling into dust. Melanie shrieked in panic. The assembly of animals swayed to the side, their balance lost. But Melanie was trying to save the disappearing dragon. The thing consuming him was now chipping away at his torso and he was reaching out to Melanie in a panicked daze. Her vision was overwhelmed with tears. The dragon gave Melanie a blank stare and then dissolved into air. The animals plummeted through the air. Sapphire caught Melanie's limp body and plopped to the ground.

"Melanie," whispered Sapphire's thoughts softly. "It's all right."

But it wasn't all right. There was someone who was making animals vanish and Melanie was always there when it happened. It wasn't all right. Unicorns are nearly extinct now. It wasn't all right. Because a dragon had just died in front of Melanie's fragile eyes.

Chapter 14
The Wall of Manipulation

Melanie had made up her mind: she was going to Merlin's, rest there for a while, go back to Riverhaven and get the feather, and then find all the vanishing animals before it was too late. So when all the other animals scuttled into the forest, thanking Melanie on the way, she had taken out her compass and marched towards Merlin's luxurious wooden apartment with a steely stone-cold emotionless mask covering her face the whole time.

As Melanie jolted to the left, following the compass, she heard Sapphire cry out in a warning. Melanie ignored her. Then, she slammed into a wall made entirely out of glass and stumbled backwards. A glass wall ... In the woods? Melanie gaped at it. She knew that there were peculiar aspects to the Trenside Thicket. But why a glass wall? An exact reflection of Melanie appeared on the other side of the wall. Except... the reflection of Melanie had an evil gleam in her eyes and she was sneering. Melanie stepped back, feeling more threatened than any of the times she had encountered a villain in the woods. An evil Melanie McGee? She couldn't imagine it.

"I am you," said the reflection.

"No," replied Melanie, keeping her trembling voice at bay.

"Melanie, for a young girl like yourself, we shouldn't be so overwhelmed with responsibilities," began the reflection. Melanie cut in:

"This isn't my responsibility. It's my choice and I am choosing to find my father and the vanishing animals."

The reflection touted.

"Oh, darling. Don't you understand? They don't want you?"

Melanie gritted her teeth in annoyance. She knew that her reflection was just trying to manipulate her. Yet... a grain of truth seemed to lie somewhere in that core of manipulation.

No one had asked her for help. She had just gone into the woods and caused more trouble. Melanie squashed down the thought.

"Your father ran away?"

Melanie's hands were shaking now, a rippling river that wouldn't stop moving. She shoved them deep below her pockets so the reflection couldn't see them.

"Just when you needed them both, Cora and Hazel disappear to let you face the truth of your father yourself.

Such horrible friends," cooed the reflection.

Melanie's eyes were now slowly turning bloodshot and her eyes welled up uncontrollably.

"You can't trust anyone but an old man that looks and acts like he's centuries old," seethed the reflection. "That must be horrible."

Melanie knew that she was being teased. You are being teased, she thought. You are being teased. You are being teased. You are being teased. YOU ARE BEING TEASED!

But all Melanie could think about was that the reflection was right: she had no more friends, no more family, just an old man. Melanie sobbed. She cried and cried until her reflection smiled cruelly.

"That's right, Melanie. You aren't meant to be here. Let the police take you. They will return you back to New York and you can just forget about everyone and everything. You won't need to face these problems anymore."

Melanie sat on the grassy floor and buried her head into her hands.

"Yeah," was al she could murmur.

"No," said a soft, gentle voice in Melanie's head. It was Sapphire. "Melanie, I trust you. Don't... go."

Melanie stopped crying. The reflection glared at Melanie blankly, her dark pupils slashing into her, asking her where her loyalties lied.

"I'm here and I'll help you," continued Sapphire's musical yet fragile voice.

"Riverhaven is out to get you," the reflection blurted, sounding desperate. That was the reflections mistake. Because nothing fuels Melanie more than stubbornness. Melanie glared at the reflection icily.

"And I'll be stopping that."

The reflection balled up its fists.

"No one wants you anymore! No one wants you!"

But Melanie had already charged at the wall, sword raised and slashed into her evil body, splintering the glass to pieces. Evil Melanie faded as the glass clinked to the ground.

"Nooooooooooo!" said the reflection, voice getting fainter and fainter until she vanished into the afternoon sky.

Chapter 15
Visiting an Old Friend

"I've been expecting you," said Merlin.

Melanie was sitting on a cushioned armchair, a bowl of golden stackaberry soup cradled in her arms.

"We have much to discuss. I know that you've gotten the feather and that your father has escaped from jail," said Merlin.

"It's all over the internet," grumbled Melanie.

"I know that Hazel and Cora have disappeared mysteriously and the animals have been as well. I'm fully aware that you've been framed for this and you ran into the woods. I'm not sure about this part, but you've most likely decided that you will get the feather, find your father, and save the animals."

"How'd you know?" intervened Melanie suspiciously.

Merlin stepped into the other room, Melanie following behind him, to reveal a frazzled and very tired looking lady.

"Natalie?" Melanie gasped.

"Melanie!"

In an instant, Melanie was wrapped in her foster mother's embrace and was sobbing the whole story into her shoulder.

"Oh my goodness, Melanie," she whispered.

The moment was interrupted by the soft purring coming from Sapphire.

"Before you go looking for your dad Melanie, you must save the animals. There is a reason why they are disappearing," said Merlin, stroking his extensively long beard.

"Then what is it, Merlin?" said Melanie, growing impatient with all of his mysterious quarrel.

"I can't tell you that. This is your story." Melanie looked at him questionably but he didn't elaborate.

"Go out to save the animals, Melanie. Then go find your father," said Merlin, his voice suddenly quitting and sounding very vulnerable.

Melanie swallowed the lump in her throat and nodded.

"Here," said Merlin, "You'll need this." He handed Melanie a bag full of random objects: goggles (for swimming,) a dog whistle, melted wax, and a couple more little trinkets. Melanie looked at him, half amused but mostly bewildered.

"You'll know when the time comes," said Merlin, smiling slyly. Melanie rolled her eyes playfully. That should be his motto, she thought. Melanie was about to head out when she remembered her foster mother.

"I'll come back for you. I promise," Melanie said to Natalie. Her foster mother wiped away the tears in her eyes and smiled weakly. Then, she collapsed Melanie into a hug.

"Be safe," she murmured through silent tears.

"Always," said Melanie. "Always."

Then, she was back into the woods.

As Melanie rubbed her eyes, washing the tears onto her palm, she tried to come up with an explanation for why someone would try to get rid of animals. To have them for his/herself? To frame Melanie? Out of fun? Nothing seemed right to Melanie and she rejected ideas as soon as they popped into her head. The problem with saving disappearing animals was: you had no idea where they disappeared to. So, wandering into the woods was the only way they could figure out where so far. When Melanie was lost in thought, she never paid attention to her surroundings, which was never a good idea when you were in the Trenside Thicket. Before Melanie could catch herself, she slipped on a log and fell face-first into a swampy green-tainted river. Melanie coughed and a string of seaweed fell out of her mouth. Sapphire giggled. Once Melanie sat up and brushed off the murky water, she peered at the winding river.

"We need to swim," choked Melanie, gagging.

Sapphire gave Melanie a *do-I-really-have-to?* look and Melanie nodded solemnly.

"I'm afraid so, Sapphire." Melanie picked out another piece of seaweed from her eyes. My eyes... Melanie thought. She dawned with understanding.

"The goggles Merlin gave me! How did he know?" she whispered, pondering the question once again. Melanie fastened the rubber band onto her head and poised towards the water.

"C'mon, Sapphire. It's time to swim."

Chapter 16
The Murky Waters of Salabashwa

Melanie hurled herself into the water and instantly came back up, choking for breath. Underneath the green, slimy surface, there was triple the amount of sludge. It was an effort to push through it and, even with her nose plugged, Melanie could smell the putrid stench of sulfur. If you didn't gag at the sight of it, then you could be the most amazing being on earth. Melanie willed herself to remember this was to save the animals and plunged deeper into the water. That was when Melanie wondered how she was going to breathe. Sapphire tapped Melanie's shoulder with her hoof.

"Breath," she said simply.

Melanie shook her head, trying to tell her that humans couldn't breath underwater without inhaling the water and ending up a giant slime ball.

"Breath," snapped Sapphire sharply.

Melanie raised her hands in a surrender. She took in a small breath. Nothing happened. She inhaled larger breaths. She could breathe!

"But... how?" she asked.

"We're entering Salabashwa," answered Sapphire gently, acting like that was the most normal thing in the world.

"What's Salashwabada?" Melanie asked.

"Salabashwa," corrected Sapphire.

Melanie nodded, still unable to pronounce the name. "Salabashwa is one of the few underwater kingdoms."

"This place is a kingdom?" marveled Melanie incredulously, "this looks more like a polluted swamp. Who lives in the kingdom?"

"Mostly just marine life," said Sapphire's hushed whisper. "But they do have a queen: Queen Salabashwa."

Melanie plunged deeper into the water, now eager to see the kingdom. Slowly, the murkiness thinned, though not completely. Angelic singing voices swallowed out the croaks of belching water. Melanie closed her eyes, taking in the soft, smooth noise. When the layer of gook cleared, Melanie saw the most awe-inspiring sight ever. A castle, shining like millions of stars and changing colors faced Melanie. It was larger than Merlin's apartment and looked too beautiful to be real. Melanie gasped. It wasn't just an ordinary castle, it was made entirely of fish! Melanie felt a happy blush tickle her skin. She was a thirteen year old girl, and was having the experience of staring at a castle of fish.

"Salabashwa." Melanie whispered under her breath, awed. Sapphire gasped as well. But it wasn't in awe. Sapphire was gasping at the colonies of fish in horror. They were turning lighter, than pale, then completely transparent in the matter of seconds. Melanie's soaring heart dropped to her stomach.

"But-But, those are just... fish."

"No. They are Salabashwanian fish," said Sapphire, "They're built entirely out of pieces of Queen Salabashwa's soul. Once all of the fishes disappear the queen will die and there won't be anything to save her."

Melanie cried out in sadness. Her shoulders bunching up and face to the ground. Melanie swam back up to the surface. Tears leaked out of her eyes. Unicorns, dragons, now fish? She wasn't going to let this happen any longer. The animals didn't deserve to die like this. Even if the rest of the world didn't want her anymore, Melanie would save the animals, getting the credit or not.

Chapter 17
The Waxed Horn

Melanie rose out of the water. She hadn't remembered the water to be cold but, as she shivered in the forest like a melting icicle, she wondered why she couldn't have found a towel first. The sun was setting and Melanie was fighting every bone in her body telling her to sleep. A happy neigh rang behind her. There was a small wooden cabin right behind the river. It hadn't been there before, Melanie swore. She drew closer, squinting suspiciously at the cabin. A sign was taped onto the front door:

I THOUGHT YOU AND SAPPHIRE WOULD WANT TO
REST.
HOPE YOU HAD A NICE SWIM
—MERLIN

Melanie smiled sheepishly. Of course Merlin would be taking care of her and Sapphire. He was probably watching her right now. Even though it was Merlin she was talking about, it sent shivers of anxiety up her spine.

"Thank you Merlin," she bellowed into the sky.

Melanie called out to Sapphire and they both trotted inside the cabin.

When Melanie had taken off the goggles, they had crumbled to dust and slipped out of Melanie's fingers. Melanie knew that was Merlin's way of guaranteeing that "you can only use it once."

The wooden cabin was complete with one comfy looking bedroom and a pile of hay (for Sapphire,) a small kitchen with food stashed in the cabinets, a TV, and a table in the living room scattered with papers. Melanie picked up one of the newspapers on the floor. It read:

Dragons are Disappearing from Riverhaven Homes

Police Scourge the Woods for Miss McGee

Melanie put the paper down, feeling crestfallen. The police were now in the woods looking for her? It was getting worse. She picked up another paper:

The Salabashwa Fish Disappearing

Queen Blames Melanie McGee for The Attacks

Melanie tore the paper to shreds, heaving sobs. Melanie knew she shouldn't read anymore, they were just more and more assumptions that would leave her heartbroken and more like a helpless fly on the wall who could only listen and never actually go out into the world. So instead, she turned on the TV, hoping there was a cartoon she should watch. Instead, a very serious and clipped man faced the camera. Behind him, there was an opening of woods and a pile of ashes that once belonged to a tree. Melanie exhaled anxiously. This had been where she escaped from Lazorus the troll.

"A young troll owning this section of the woods has been collecting animals for a mythical creature sanctuary," began the reporter. Melanie scowled. Lazarus had been doing no such thing. Lazarus, the smelly and bearded troll in the forest was doing pretty much the opposite before Melanie stopped him. "Then, the traitor that we all know of as Melanie McGee, vanishing our animals, came and burned down the place, taking all the innocent sanctuary animals with her." Melanie's mouth dropped as low as her heart. A single tear rolled down her cheek. That lying-lying thief! The reporter stuck the microphone and bent down to Lazaros, who was wiping fake tears with a muddy handkerchief.

"Melanie came and burned my animals to crisps," fake-sobbed Lazorus. "She's- she-s a monster!"

Melanie slammed the TV remote, turning the TV off. Melanie's hand grazed one last newspaper. Even though Melanie willed herself not to, she read it. The contents nearly knocked her off her feet:

Sightings of Two Girls Screaming for Help in The South Woods

Who is to blame?

Melanie had no proof, but she was sure those two girls were Hazel and Cora. They had been kidnapped! Melanie's jaw was sct. She was going to figure out who framed her and then save her friends. Now. Melanie thought of all the enemies she had made throughout her life. She jotted them down on a torn newspaper.

- Lazorus the Troll, though I met him after I was framed
- King Henry of The Monerines
- My reflection, though I met her after I was framed
- Ashley
- That boy at Merlin's house
- Any jealous person in Riverhaven or the world

There were so many possibilities. She ran the list

through her head. It couldn't have been Lazorus or the reflection; she had come to know them after she had been framed. King Henry of The Monerines. That was a possibility. While Melanie had fled into the woods, he had parted with the last words of:

"You will pay for this, Melanie! You'll see. One day you will regret what you've done!"

Was this how he was getting his revenge on her? By turning the world against her? It did sound like something he would do. But Melanie couldn't be sure. He didn't seem clever enough. Ashley. When Melanie had befriended Hazel and Cora, another girl named Ashley with orange hair and freckles had taken a dislike to Melanie and was jealous of some connection that she had. No, Melanie thought. That's too much work for someone with such a little cause. That boy at Merlin's house. The boy named Oliver that Melanie had seen glaring at her in Merlin's house was probably least likely to frame her than Ashley. Melanie shot down the idea. The only conclusion Melanie had come to was any jealous person in Riverhaven or the world. But there were so many people in the world and interviewing every single one would take a lifetime. Melanie didn't have much time to think because Sapphire ran into the room, screaming, or neighing in distress, as loud as a unicorn could. She was disappearing.

"No," Melanie rasped, going sickly pale. "No!" But

Sapphire's leg was already completely gone, crumbling to invisible dust. Melanie didn't know what to do but scream.

"Sapphire! No!!"

Her other leg was gone. What could she do? Sapphire's waist was gone! What could she do? Melanie remembered the bag Merlin had given to her. A pair of goggles, a dog whistle and... liquid wax.

Her goggles were gone, the dog whistle didn't seem like much use, but... the wax? Sapphire's neck was now fading away. Melanie choked on tears and the lump in her throat that wouldn't swallow. Where was the wax? She scrambled around the room, knocking vases and shattering glass everywhere. WHERE WAS THE WAX? Sapphire's chin was gone, a head only remaining. Lips. Nose. Eyes. Melanie slipped on a vial and thudded to the floor, a bottle of wax rolling by her. She found it! Melanie scurried to Sapphire, the only thing remaining of her, a hovering horn. Melanie spilled the molten lava-hot wax on the horn and stuck her hand in the burning-gooey mixture. It ate at her flesh but Melanie swallowed the pain. She was stuck to Sapphire. Slowly, along with her unicorn's, her hand started to disappear, then her arm, then her legs. Until Melanie and Sapphire were gone, the only thing remaining was a vial of glass, slowly turning to dust.

Chapter 18
The Vanishings Again

Melanie's palm was scorching hot. Her skin was peeling, revealing raw and unprepared flesh. Melanie had closed her eyes forcefully, waiting for the moment when she couldn't open them anymore. But when her feet landed softly onto cold mud, she was able to open them. She was standing in a long tunnel, smelling like dew and wet air. Melanie went to scratch her itching chin when she saw that her hand was still glued to Sapphire's horn. But it wasn't just a horn anymore. It was her full body!

"Oh Sapphire," Melanie gasped, "You-you're... alive!" Sapphire smiled weakly, seeming surprised herself. Melanie reached out to hug her, ripping the wax, making them each wince in pain, and embrace each other. Like always, it was interrupted with a small whisper in Melanie's head. This time, it wasn't smooth like Sapphire's but raspy and defeated, like she was its last hope.

"Please," it croaked, "save us from him. Or we'll all die."

Him?

"Please," it repeated, "The world's turning black. No...

You're too late."

A hoarse scream rang through Melanie's ears. Then, the voice disappeared entirely. Melanie shuddered and a dry sob ripped through her throat. Whatever she had heard was enough to make anyone break down into tears, at least if they had gone through all the trauma she had experienced. Another scream, this time louder echoed like a bell in her ears. Melanie launched herself forward. More screams. Louder. Louder. She sprung into action. Hurdling onto Sapphire's back, (which must've hurt) she let her gallop into the winding tunnel. More screams. What was going on? The tunnel got narrower and the air thinned. Melanie coughed, gasping for breaths. Sapphire was wheezing uncontrollably and Melanie had to get off of her back before her unicorn would pass out completely. They slowly prowled down the dirt-paved road. The farther they went in, the shallower their breaths became and the darker the tunnel seemed. A hissy laugh came from behind them. Melanie sprung around, her arms wildly flailing in the pitch black tunnel, grasping nothing. The laugh came again but this time, next to her. Melanie clutched her skin where her furiously beating heart lay beneath. She couldn't think under the roaring thumps of her heart, warning her to turn around and leave. But even if she wanted to, Melanie couldn't find the exit anymore. It was too dark. Sapphire's horn glowed hot pink, indicating that she was scared. Melanie ran forward, her only solution for getting out of the tunnel and... found herself standing in a massive dirt room, completely empty except for a long marble lever on the other side, pushed into the wall like it had been hurriedly put in there. Melanie lifted her quaking leg and stepped towards it. The hissing laugh spiraled around the room. Melanie looked around, breathing heavily and biting her lip in fear. She ran to the other side of the room and jerked the lever forward, opening a titanic slit in the dirt wall, and crawled through with Sapphire before it closed. She sighed in relief. The sighs slowly turned to choked gasps when she saw where she sat. Around every corner that Melanie looked, there were animals, or more specifically: Riverhaven animals, all a soft translucent and sometimes fading as if they were glitching computers.

"The vanishing animals," Melanie breathed.

She walked around, not even trying to prevent the droplets falling out of her eyes as she watched the animals claw at their circular prisons.

"Melanie," whispered a croaking voice in her head. Melanie turned. It was the dragon that had helped the others escape from Lazorus, the one that had saved her, the one she thought was dead. Melanie's spirits soared.

Melanie had never given it a name.

"Briarried!" she swallowed. Melanie hadn't thought

when she said the name, but it felt right.

She was about to ask him why he hadn't escaped when the door was just open, when Sapphire screamed in warning. Melanie jumped. Facing her, was a man with slick grey hair and gleaming grass green eyes, who looked dangerously like Melanie's father.

Chapter 19
The Woods Master

"**I** see you've met my pets," hissed the man.

Melanie blanched, the voice completely ripped out of her. "Y-you... animals. You took them. Father? Bu-but." Melanie rasped, her sentences laying unformed.

The man smiled. He resembled Melanie's father quite a bit. Same hair, though more of it; same gleam in the eyes, though more evil looking.

"Who are you?" Melanie managed to croak.

"Why, I'm flattered by your curiosity," the man mocked for no particular reason. "I am the Woods Master."

"I haven't heard of you," Melanie retorted. Silently, Melanie cursed her big mouth. Her small problem was that she had a tendency to blurt whatever was on her mind, no matter the circumstances. Take the time she had nearly been attacked by Monerines as an example, she had asked their leader, King Henry:

"King of what? Dead fish?"

That hadn't ended well. The Woods Master hissed

dangerously.

"Do you see these animals here, Melanie? The ones you spent so long to get to?"

"Of course," Melanie began to say. But the animals were gone. She had seen them moments ago! "What-what did you do?" she rasped.

"What do you mean?" he teased, "The animals are right here." Melanie glared at him, ready to justify him for his lies but... the second that she had looked away, the animals were back.

Melanie gaped, unable to move.

"Oh," the Woods Master said with fake astonishment, "they're gone again." Melanie clenched her fists. How was he doing that?

"He's sending us to Riverhaven and then returning us again back here," sang the voice of a unicorn in Melanie's head. All the puzzle pieces clicked for Melanie, even though she still didn't know how this man was doing what he was doing. Melanie thanked the voice and thought of a plan in her head.

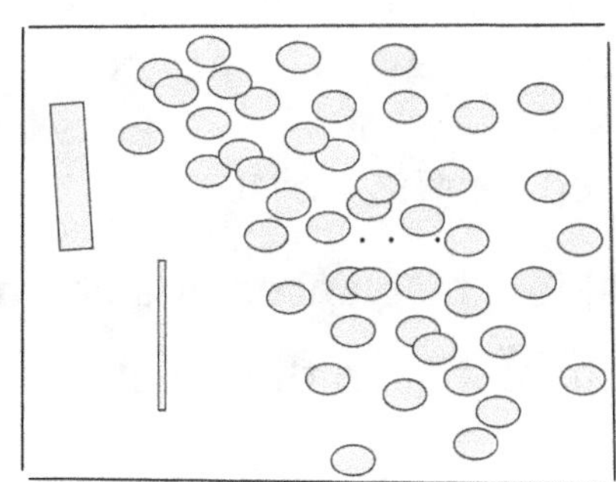

If all the animals (circles) are scattered all over the place, Melanie thought, how was she going to grab all of them at once? The Woods Master smiled cruelly at her.

"I've heard rumors throughout the woods that you can hear animals's thoughts and wishes, you are quite a legend," the man hissed in his throaty voice. It sent snowstorms of prickly cold unease through Melanie's body. There's nothing worse in the world than some weird snake-sounding guy knowing everything about you.

"People talk about me?" was the only thing she managed to say.

"Most definitely, yes." he whispered, his mouth barely even moving.

"And your Bond is working with animals. Mythical animals," he said, acting like each word was a separate sentence, emphasizing each one. "My bond is much like your fa-ther's" he said, "His is re-venge, while mine is po-wer."

"What are you doing with these animals?" Melanie seethed.

"I guess I can tell you," he said, "you would e-ven-tua-lly find out."

Melanie prepared for the worst.

Instead of speaking, he glanced at a normal whiteboard filled with notes that hadn't been there before.

Plan to Take the Woods

Start: Get Rid of The Animals

Part 2: Blame Miss McGee

Part 3: Vanish Riverhaven

Part 4: ...

Melanie didn't continue reading. This man was trying to rule the woods, that part was clear. Melanie guessed there were some crazy villains that had tried stuff like this before, but this... Woods Master was definitely different. He was out for more power. And before he did, he was going to let Riverhaven disappear completely. Melanie's head whirred in fear and her stomach jolted side to side. He was trying to get rid of her town. The thing that runs her life. Melanie felt downright sick. But why get rid of Riverhaven?

The Woods Master read her thoughts.

"Melanie, if you'd like to know why it's Riverhaven I seek to destroy, then you should go to Merlin and ask him for The Book. He's been hiding something from you."

Melanie's blood boiled. Merlin had been hiding something? She didn't doubt it, he was slightly irritating with his mysterious phrases in the first place. This was starting to get aggravating. Melanie stopped short. This was a murderous villain she was listening to. She would think about Merlin later and not let this Tree Dude control her.

"You see, Melanie. The animals that are disappearing were only the first phase of my plan. I can only vanish Riverhaven completely if the townsfolk lose faith in their mythical animals. The mythical animals are the only thing that anchors Riverhaven to reality. Without its animals, Riverhaven would sweep away out of history like dandelion fluff breezing through the wind." Melanie stammered in disbelief.

For one thing, I'd like to point out how dumb I think telling your plan to a girl who has the potential to stop him is. It's like saying: I'm going to put your birthday presents on top of the closet, you can sneak a peek. And if he had to tell her his plans, could he at least have been dramatic about it? Well, it is what it is... The Woods Master still hadn't answered the million dollar question though: Why Riverhaven?

Chapter 20
The Final Vanishing

Melanie was going to ask her question again when another question popped in her head:

"How are you making everything vanish?"

She didn't expect much of an answer but he gave it to her willingly. He smiled his horrible smile and waved his hands. Suddenly, and I mean suddenly, thousands of ghostly grey dogs appeared from thin air, circling the animals, vanishing and reappearing every other second.

Melanie gasped.

"Only known in the deepest of legends and history, the spirit dogs are symbols of incredible power. They are fierce enough to tear any of the animals to shreds if they dare move. Their power can overthrow entire villages, like vanishing Riverhaven entirely," recited The Woods Master in his merciless proud way. Melanie's gut twisted with dread.

"Now, off to Riverhaven!!" he roared. Half of the ghostly dogs drowned in the air, leaving only a trail of marene blue hovering in the air, pointing towards the direction of the town. The rest of the dogs prowled closer to the animals, drooling through their spiked teeth gnashing threateningly. For a fraction of a second, Melanie saw Merlin's glowing face appear. It dissipated as soon as it came. The dog whistle! Of course! Melanie flung her satchel off her back and clutched the whistle like a dagger. Would it work on magical dogs as well? There was only one way to figure it out. She blew all the air out of her lungs into the silver whistle.

The Woods Master stood still like a statue and then laughed and laughed. Then, all of a sudden all the dogs ran around in different directions, bumping into the caged animals and accidentally freeing them, causing bursts of chaos in every place they departed to. Melanie smiled. The animals were free, now she just had to deal with the infuriated villain in front of her. The mythical creatures sprinted out of the door, glad to leave their horrors behind, some murmuring a quick thank you on the way. The Woods Master howled in frustration.

He thrust his hand forward and a rope bound Melanie to the ground.

"Before anything else happens Melanie I want to show you the queen of Salabshwa. You see she lives in her castle but her spirit and soul are in her fish. If all her fish vanish then she is gone forever. And it works the same way for Riverhaven. The soul of Riverhaven is in their animals. They might be free but the townsfolk are in a crisis. They're pretty little animals have been gone for so long that they don't believe in them any more. So much that Riverhaven is going to disappear all on its own. Like the queen. Because she just lost all her fish. Once Riverhaven is gone, she and everyone else will disappear forever."

Melanie was speechless. Her nightmare was a reality.

"You may have gotten half of my spirit dogs to fail but the rest are in Riverhaven, making it vanish at this very moment. It would be a pity if you couldn't go along with it," he growled menacingly. Melanie thrashed at her binds desperately, kicking and pulling. She looked around for Sapphire but couldn't find her anywhere.

"Bye bye savior of the town," mocked the Woods Master. Melanie screamed shrillily. Her leg turned invisible.

"Help!"

Her waist was gone.

"Please!" she cried.

Her lips crumbled to dust. And then, she was in Riverhaven. But it didn't look like Riverhaven at all, half consumed by the vanishing power of the spirit dogs with the other half switched into chaos mode with screaming people, running around and clutching their younger ones. No one even noticed Melanie. Her full body was back but she could only lay limp and rigid as a rag doll on the soft paved sidewalk. The town was crumbling, and it looked as if it was drifting away. Dissolving.

"Please! Somebody free me. I can help!" Melanie cried, her voice starting to turn hoarse. Horror pierced her insides when she saw what she was actually lying on. Beneath her, the cement was slowly dissipating. If it got any closer, it would take her with it and permanently dissolve Melanie forever.

"No!" a female voice cried. In a flash, Natalie was dashing towards her, emerald eyes wide and stricken.

"Natalie," Melanie sobbed in relief.

With a blunt knife, Natalie cut and cut through the binds. The floor beneath Melanie's pants was crumbling.

"Natalie!" Melanie cried louder. The knife made its final cut and slashed through the binds. Melanie leapt up and landed safely on the other side, a second away from being banished forever.

"My daughter!" Natalie weeped in a mixture of sadness and relief. A young boy clinging to a disappearing statue cried out and Melanie snapped back to attention.

"We have to save the town!" Meline wheezed, the realization that Riverhaven was going to die finally settling in. No matter how many times she had thought it before, it just didn't seem real until that real human boy had just disappeared. That would happen to everyone here. And the feather! No, this was too dangerous.

"Round up the animals! Natalie said, "they're our only hope." How had she known? thought Melanie. She pushed the thought down. Save the town, then ask questions.

"SAPPHIRE!" Melanie called. At the exact same time, Natalie whistled a complicated tune. Sapphire came bounding in, leading the unicorns. Then the rest of the animals poured in.

"How did you do that?" Meline asked, staring in amazement at Natalic.

"Later!" she shouted

"Animals," Melanie rasped, "The world depends on the faith people have in you. When your loyalty vows to Riverhaven forever, the people will see that you haven't left us."

"You have to believe!" Natalie added, coming up behind Melanie. "You have to believe that the town is here."

Talk about being cheesy.

Inside Melanie's head, a couple voices whispered:

"We vow to protect Riverhaven! We vow to protect Riverhaven! We vow to protect Riverhaven!"

"Louder!" Melanie said.

"We vow to protect Riverhaven! We vow to protect Riverhaven! We vow to protect Riverhaven!"

The voices weren't in Melanie's head anymore, they were coming out of the animal's lips and echoing through the chaos. The townsfolk turned in awe and surprise. The screams seemed to die down and no one was paying attention to the vanishing floors anymore.

"WE VOW TO PROTECT RIVERHAVEN! WE VOW TO PROTECT RIVERHAVEN! RIVERHAVEN!"

Melanie closed her eyes, letting the chanting swirl around her. She remembered walking through the zoo, riding dragons, conversing with Griffins. She remembered the feel of the magic of the town. Riverhaven was real!

The crumbling walls stopped crumbling. The boy clinging to the statue cheered. Riverhaven was slowly reforming again!

"WE VOW TO PROTECT RIVERHAVEN! WE VOW TO PROTECT RIVERHAVEN! RIVERHAVEN!"

It wasn't just the animals now. The townsfolk had joined in!

A Spirit dog roared but it was drowned out by cheers. Another dog reached its paw out to slash at Melanie but, when it touched, it dissipated to dirt. Hugs went all around the crowd, tears and sniffles were passed along. Riverhaven was saved!

Melanie sat down on a bench, easing the twister of emotions in her stomach. She breathed, positively exhausted. Questions swirled through her mind. Where was her father? Where was Merlin? Where was the Woods Master? But as she breathed out her worries, the last question in her head remained: Why was Riverhaven the Woods Master wanted?

Melanie felt her eyes fall, ready to sleep. People had gone back to their homes. Construction workers were coming tomorrow to fix up the damage. So many lives had been lost this time. Humans and animals had disappeared forever. This would be an impact that would harm the economy for years to come. Sitting on her wooden bench, she got ready to fall asleep right there. Just then, with a loud crack, the cunning face of the Woods Master hovered above Melanie's startled expression. She took a step back, ready to call for help, when she realized he was just a projection.

"Wh-what are you doing here?" she spluttered

The Woods Master laughed and hissed playfully. "Hello Melanie," he drawled. He was dressed in a casual suit with the same cruel smile on his lips.

"I just wanted to congratulate you," he said, pretending to be oblivious to her obvious growing confusion and rage. "You managed to stop me, much to my surprise. But be warned, this is just the beginning."

"What makes you so sure?" asked Melanie boldly.

He hissed again. The horrible noise sent shivers down Melanie's spine. "Because Melanie, I have your father. And you wouldn't want to leave him behind, would you?"

Then he disappeared with a crack, the last she ever saw of the Woods Master being his evil smile.

Part 3

Chapter 21
The Trenside Thicket

Natalie took pride in many things: her fearlessness, her athletics, her kindness, and her talent for soothing people when they were hurt emotionally. But when Melanie ran into the house, blubbering like a four-year-old and grabbing a bag full of clothes and food, Natalie's talent for soothing vanished.

"Melanie! What's wrong?"

Melanie stared at her blankly for a moment and then continued her weeping.

"Melanie!" Natalie snapped, growing increasingly worried, "What's. Wrong?"

Melanie gaped at her and choked out the words with so much pain, it looked like she just wanted to die:

"He's-he's-he's got my daaaad!" Natalie blanched the color of bleach. Just hours ago, a man called the Woods Master had used rare magical dogs that were long forgotten to try and vanish Riverhaven into thin air. And, now, Melanie had just explained that the same man had captured her father.

"I'm-I'm going into the T-Trenside Th-Thicket." stammered Melanie, tears dripping off of her delicate eyelashes.

"No! It's dangerous," blurted Natalie.

Melanie glared at her. "What do you know about the Trenside Thicket?"

"When I heard that you were in the woods running from the police, I went after you and found Merlin, who brought me back home. But I had an encounter with a couple... dangers." She shuddered, though seaking to rapidly for a normal answer. Melanie stared, dumbfounded. Natalie hadn't told her that. She knew that she was at Merlin's, of course. She had been there as well. But Melanie also knew full awareness how dangerous The Trenside Thicket was, she had made too many enemies in there.

"Did you get hurt?" inquired Melanie, packing various sweaters, pants and undergarments into her satchel.

"No," answered Natalie quickly, though they both knew she was lying.

"Well, I'm going to save my father, and hopefully find Hazel and Cora on the way," replied Melanie stubbornly.

Hazel and Cora had been Melanie's only human friends before they had been kidnapped. Melanie had decided it was the Woods Master, mostly as an assumption but also because of a newspaper she had found in a cabin by the waters of Salabashwa.

Sightings of Two Girls Screaming for Help in The South Woods.

Who is to blame?

The South Woods was exactly where the Woods Master's cave had been located. Melanie flung the satchel onto her back and marched out the door.

"See you when I save father, Natalie," she declared, wiping tears from her cheek.

"Now wait a minute," said Natalie, "You really think that you're going to parade into the woods without me being there?"

"I did it the two other times I went into the Thicket," replied Melanie persistently.

"But those times you didn't have me around asking to come as well," retorted Natalie calmly. Melanie folded her arms and grumped, knowing she had lost. She knew she wasn't getting rid of Natalie.

Melanie snatched a piece of paper from the floor and started scribbling down a plan:

Find Feather = Melanie

Go into the Thicket and scream Briarriedes into the air =
Natalie

Melanie thought for a moment, wondering what else could be added to the plan. She thought back to the present Merlin had given to her friend, Hazel. Melanie squealed, an idea dawning on her.

Escape from the woods = Hazel and Cora

Natalie looked at Melanie, puzzled.

"Who is Briarried?" she asked.

Melanie didn't answer.

"And you know dear that Cora and Hazel are kidnapped. How do you think they will get out? And why would you add it to the plan?"

Melanie smiled at her foster mother mysteriously. "You'll see," she said.

Natalie shook her head, laughing to herself.

Melanie began wrapping the paper up but stopped. Something else was nagging at the back of her mind. She remembered the conversation she had with The Woods Master and added to the list:

Find out what "The Book" is = Melanie (though later in the journey)

143

"Off we go," said Melanie, springing into action.

"Off we go," murmured Natalie, departing in the opposite direction, towards the Trenside Thicket.

Chapter 22
The Feather, the Dragon, and the Note

Melanie was dashing through the town square, a long black cloak draped over her body. Melanie's name had been mostly cleared when she helped save Riverhaven. But there were still some townsfolk looking for her and waiting for the exact moment when they could call the police and get rid of her once and for all. That's when the cloak had come in.

The metal feather that Melanie was going to had been locked up in a box and buried below the Riverhaven zoo, now completely abandoned. When her father had escaped from jail, she had been planning on getting the feather and using it to find him. But since then, a lot has happened. On her way to the feather, she had been accused of vanishing animals and was chased by police all the way into the woods. It wasn't going to happen again. Melanie slowly opened the unused door to the zoo with a crack and tiptoed inside. Floorboards tethered to the side as she walked. She looked to the side. All clear. Then, she scampered outside and started digging through the ground with her bare hands. It was unpleasant, but it had to be done. At last, the metal safe appeared out of the dirt. Melanie lightly caressed the scrunchie in her hair. Usually, she wore it on her wrist, but today was an exception. She wanted her hair out of her eyes. Unbeknownst to most people, Melanie, being a quick learner, had begged Natalie to teach her to sow, about a year ago. Learning swiftly, she had soon grown into an exceptional sower, and had signed the code of the safe right into the scrunchie. There was no need to open it now, she knew the code by heart. She approached the safe and punched 3-8-7-7-2-4 into the keypad. The safe opened with a crack. Melanie smiled. She had gone on other life-risking missions that broke her heart in millions of pieces. This one would be easy. She'd have the feather, free her friends, talk to her father, and be able to rest with no more overwhelming problems.

Her thoughts receded. There was going to be no saving and resting anytime soon. No one would be finding this easy anymore. Because the feather wasn't there, just a tattered note waiting for Melanie to unfold it.

Natalie carefully whispered into Sapphire's ear, (Melanie's unicorn) "Look after Melanie please," and then sprinted into the woods, forcing herself not to look back. Her foster daughter had written down what she was supposed to do: run into the woods and scream Briarrides into the air. Most parents would have found it ridiculous that she was taking orders from her foster daughter. Even more so, that she was ordered to scream a random name in the air. Nevertheless, Natalie would do it. She had other duties and she wanted to get them done. Doing one favor for Melanie would be fine. Natalie tripped on her navy cloak. Melanie had insisted that they both wear the cloth above themselves, claiming that if they didn't, they would be arrested in a second.

By the time Natalie had arrived at the edge of the woods, she was panting like a hog, dripping with sweat from the dark cloak absorbing the rays of the steaming sun. Natalie swept the cloak off of herself and delved deep into the woods. Natalie suddenly felt very pathetic. She had let her foster daughter roam through a town with some people that still wanted her arrested. Her palms started sweating increasingly, faster than before. Why wasn't Melanie back yet? She needed her. How long did it take to grab a feather and run? Melanie had written:

Escape from the woods = Hazel and Cora

Melanie knew that Hazel and Cora were trapped, so why had she written that? Was Melanie going mad from the sadness? Natalie chuckled nervously. Of course not! Just scream Briarrides and then worry about what happens next, Natalie demanded herself. "Alright then, but you'll regret it," said a small voice in Natalie's head. She squashed it down.

"Briarrides!" Natalie screeched, hoping no one in the

town had heard her. She flushed with embarrassment.

Nothing was happening. Did Melanie's plan fail? Natalie flung her cloak back on her sweat covered shirt. Nothing had happened. Melanie would eventually mess up, she thought. It's alright. But just when she prepared to leave the forest, a thundering dragon swept through the air, spewing smoke.

Chapter 23
The Letter

Melanie's head swarmed with panic. The feather was gone! Her heart thumped at the same pace of her pounding thoughts. Feather gone. A note in the safe. Where is the feather? Who wrote the note? Am I in danger? This is really bad. Melanie squatted to the ground, trembling hands unfolding the note. Her heart stopped. She recognized that handwriting. The handwriting that was like a million sardines trying to fit in one can. The note was from her father!

Dearest Melanie, she read, heart clenching and unclenching when she thought about what he wrote next.

You can not imagine how much I missed you. I know you think that I betrayed you and that I escaped from jail out of my own free will. But you're wrong. I'm sorry, He forced me to.

Melanie's face reddened with rage. She already knew who her father was talking about... The Woods Master.

When you came to visit me in jail, he forced me to steal the code of numbers in your scrunchie, memorize it, put it back, and then take the feather.

Melanie seethed as she read, tears dripping on the paper and smearing some of the ink. Melanie remembered the last time she visited her father, before he escaped. Walter had touched Melanie's wrist gently, fingers lightly caressing the space below her scrunchie. That was when he had taken the string of numbers! And Melanie hadn't even noticed.

I left this note to you when he wasn't looking, knowing you would come for the feather. You need to stop him. And you must act quickly. I must tell you something of extreme importance. Make sure you read this part alone. For days, I have been spying on the Woods Master, (through the cell that he locked me in) attempting to divulge his plan. I only got one part out, you have a spy in your mist. A mole. One you are very close to.

A spy? Melane's heart skipped a beat. Who? The next part of the letter was sloppier, as if her father had been in a hurry.

This spy is an incredibly amazing actress, and a master of deception. This person started truly caring about you but the Woods Master changed the person's mind. I'm sorry Melanie, but the Woods Master says you have grown close to her and I can't let you be endangered. You must severe contact with her immediately! She is exceptionally dangerous!!! She goes by the name—Natalie.

Chapter 24
Briarrides

Melanie jolted upwards, legs turning to jello and her posture unsteadying and swaying to the side, speechless. She took in what she read. No. She refused to believe it. Her legs lost their balance and she collapsed to the dirt. Pain flooded her legs but she didn't pay any attention to it. Doubts clouded her thoughts. Natalie would never betray her to the Woods Master, would she? Her father could be wrong. MY FATHER COULD BE WRONG, she thought, the words sounding more desperate as each word thumped inside of her. Please let it be that her father was wrong. Melanie didn't like getting sentimental. It took away her time to think of plans and the thoughts of how to survive. She had gotten emotional too many times during her journey for Riverhaven. But the more she thought about the letter, the harder it became to hold in the tears. They eventually pooled out of her, leaving the emerald eyes that usually illuminated her face, bloodshot and streaked with tears. She crumpled the letter until it was as small as a tiny ball of aluminum foil. Melanie buried it deep below in her pocket. Her thoughts wavered to all the possibilities. Natalie good, Natalie evil. Dad right, dad wrong. The thoughts then suddenly switched to the future. Would she allow Natalie to continue with her on the journey? If she said no, Natalie would be on to her. But would she want a dangerous person with her on her small quest? How much would she be able to tell Natalie? Then, the worst question hit her. How would she be able to live with a spy? Melanie's heart froze and shattered like tiny icicles. She was only thirteen and these thoughts were running through her mind. A wrenching dread churned in her stomach like butter. Her gut spoke to her with a decision. She would stay with Natalie but tell her nothing.

***

"Woah," breathed Natalie, watching as the majestic dragon thumped to the ground and puffed one more cloud of smoke out of its flaring nostrils. The dragon looked around and softened when he saw Natalie. She smiled weakly. Natalie reached out to touch him when, at that same moment, Melanie came sprinting in, Sapphire at her heels, screaming:

"No! Don't touch him!"

Natalie recoiled back, shocked. She looked at Melanie, the question shining through her eyes. Melanie straightened and cleared her throat, pushing the sudden fear out of her stomach. For a moment, her throat clogged up and the rising lump of horror wouldn't budge from its stubborn position.

After many coughs, Melanie spoke. "Um ... Briarrides is very shy. He...uh... isn't used to new people." Briarrides huffed in disapproval. Natalie gave Melanie a suspicious look but she pretended like she didn't notice it and hid her clammy hands behind her back.

"Briarrides owes me a favor," said Melanie, looking away from the possible spy, "I helped free him twice. Since Sapphire can't hold both of our weight, I thought Briarrides could help us out." Natalie nodded, smiling. Melanie didn't return it.

"Hey Briarrides," Melanie said, trying to squeeze the awkward tension that had built up between the three, "Could you fly Natalie please? I'll go on Sapphire until she's too tired." Briarrides nodded his head, at least as much as a dragon could. The truth was, Melanie was stalling all the time so she didn't have to be close to Natalie. But forcing Sapphire to fly for a time that she couldn't manage wasn't kind nor safe. The last time Melanie had pushed her unicorn's limits, she had nearly died falling into the Hudson River. Melanie wiped her sweat-stopped palms on her shirt and jumped onto Sapphire's back. Natalie glanced back at Melanie, brows furrowed. Melanie ignored it.

"Where are we going exactly?" Natalie asked.

"That hasn't been decided yet," Melanie answered coldly, her feelings towards Natalie changed by the letter she had read minutes ago.

"You know Melanie, I could help with figuri—"

Melanie cut Natalie off sharply. "I know what I'm doing, Natalie," she snapped, voice rising. Natalie reeled back, astonished. She couldn't ever remember a time when Melanie had acted so rash towards her. Natalie sighed, reluctantly.

"Alright then," she puffed, turning away and then glancing back, worried.

"Good," she said, "Let's go."

Melanie's head swarmed like a nest of buzzing bees. I can do this, she thought. I've gotten this far. But the truth was, Melanie felt alone and even more scared. She didn't want Natalie to be siding with the Woods Master. After her father had disappeared, Natalie had become her only family left. But Melanie wasn't only feeling this way because of her personal liking to her foster mother, but more because caging up all these raw and hungry feelings that clawed at her heart, was impossible. That was when they occasionally leaked out, like when she had snapped at Natalie for not much of a reason but that her feelings needed to escape. Deep down, Melanie knew that she couldn't lead her third quest into the dangerous woods with dangerous villains like a fully grown, mature adult. She was only thirteen after all. Plus, Natalie's worried looks were softening her by the minute as she flew through the air atop Sapphire. "See," Melanie told the negative side of her brain, "Natalie wouldn't side with The Woods Master if she's worried about me."

This spy is an incredibly amazing actress, and a master of deception, echoed Walter's printed words in Melanie's head. *An incredibly amazing actress.* Was everything Natalie doing just an act?

"Of course!" answered the negative side of her brain, "It's staring you down in the face." Melanie squished the voice down like how she always had to. How was it possible that her thoughts kept drifting away from the task at hand? Save Hazel, Cora, her father, arrest the Woods Master, and then think about Natalie, she thundered to her wavering thoughts. Melanie reviewed the plan in her head that she had written before she left. As her brain mentally walked through it, she added bold marks to what she needed to do next:

Find Feather = Melanie **N/A Anymore**

Go into the Thicket and scream Briarriedes into the air=Natalie **Check!**

Escape from the woods= Hazel and Cora **To do that, Briarrides needs to land on the floor and I will need to get him to perform "the ritual"**

Find out what "The Book" is= Melanie (though later in the journey) **Confront Merlin sometime during the journey**

Melanie scratched at her head, a pain in her forehead slowly building up and clogging her thoughts. Bitterly, Melanie wrote one last word in her head to the plan.

Survive!

Chapter 25
"The Ritual"

The four questers didn't land to the ground as smoothly as they wished. First, Melanie had kicked the side of Sapphire's furry body gently, telling her to delve down to the ground. Sapphire had understood and began the drop downwards. But like every unicorn that had a companion: she was an incredible show-off. Trying to impress Melanie, Sapphire had swooped down and flipped through the air. But, as one of the mistakes that she had made before, Sapphire had underestimated the weight of a thirteen-year-old girl. Halfway through the twirl in the air, Sapphire lost balance and the two plunged down towards the trees, hanging upside down through the air.

But that wasn't the biggest problem. Melanie, who after a traumatizing experience of hanging over The Hudson River from one dangling unicorn hoof, millions of feet up in the air, had become extremely afraid of heights. She could endure small flying on a dragon or unicorn. But Melanie hadn't prepared for such a drop in the air. Her stomach flipped like pancakes over and over again until she could feel

156

the breakfast she had eaten rise close to her throat. Melanie swallowed it and panicked. And since, Melanie, who, under pressure, acted without thinking, thrashed and loosened her grip from Sapphire until she had unclinged from her completely, pummeling at an extreme rate towards the ground with no unicorn or Hudson River to save her. How did she always end up pummeling towards her death in her little missions, she thought? First, when facing her father's dragon. Then, when she had dangled above New York City.

And now, about to die in The Trenside Thicket. Briarides had then swooped down, trying to save his friend. But he, being of extreme weight, had just crashed face forward, luckily managing to grab Melanie in the process. But, in the whole moment of danger, they hadn't realized that the hulking Briarrides that had saved Melanie, was falling towards a tree. Before Briarides could lift himself back into a steady pace in the air, they crashed into the tree, listening as the branches splintered and a loud crack echoed through the forest. Natalie and Melanie groaned. And the whole time, as Melanie had scolded herself for her rational actions, Sapphire had landed to the ground, gingerly and not a scratch etched into her skin.

Once the chaotic and swirling of her stomach eased, Melanie finally remembered why she had wanted to land in the first place: Cora and Hazel. Just after the three girls had met, they had come up with a silly, playful dance that they had called "the ritual." It involved a series of foot taps, jumps, hand clapping motions, and roars. They had come up with it when Merlin had given them a present that had to do with their bond. Each part of the ritual represented something different such as Cora's bond (swordplay,) Melanie's bond (bonding with animals,) and Hazel's bond (the pendant/trusting everyone and finding the good in people). When Melanie had been brainstorming furiously for how to free them, a genius idea popped into her head. Hopefully, Hazel and Cora would understand it too. Melanie strode past Natalie, not even glancing at her and charged up to Briarrides, hands on her hip and glancing into the distance like a member of a regal court. She felt powerful, almost like a king. But she knew that the power wouldn't last long, so she tried to hold on to it as much as she could.

"Briarrides, would you mind and perform the ritual for me?" said Melanie, asking it as a form of question but making it clear with her glare that it was an order.

Briarrides narrowed his eyes, confused.

Melanie flushed crimson with embarrassment. "Oh... um... right. I guess I need to show it to you." Melanie felt comfortable performing "the ritual" with her friends. But doing it in front of a dragon and a supposed spy made her face feel hot. She cleared her throat awkwardly and began dancing. *Tap. Tap. Roar. Clap. Tap. Roar, Clap. Tap. Tap.* Then, she did it again. *Tap. Tap. Roar. Clap. Tap. Roar, Clap. Tap. Tap.*

After stopping and shuffling her hands around awkwardly, he nodded to Briarrides, indicating for him to do it as well. Melanie's plan was simple: Briarides was a massive dragon, big enough to flatten all the trees around him if he wished. When he performed "the ritual" it would surely be heard all throughout the forest, including where Hazel and Cora were tied up. Hopefully, Hazel would understand what she was indicating when she hears it. Briarrides began: *Tap. Tap. Roar. Clap. Tap. Roar, Clap. Tap. Tap. Tap. Tap. Roar. Clap. Tap. Roar, Clap. Tap. Tap. Tap. Tap. Roar. Clap. Tap. Roar, Clap. Tap. Tap. Tap. Tap. Roar. Clap. Tap. Roar, Clap. Tap. Tap.*

Chapter 26
The Locket

Tap. Tap. Roar. Clap. Tap. Roar, Clap. Tap. Tap.

"Do you hear that?" asked Cora.

Tap. Tap. Roar. Clap. Tap. Roar, Clap. Tap. Tap. Hazel paused for a moment. *Tap. Tap. Roar. Clap. Tap. Roar, Clap. Tap. Tap.* "I do," she answered.

Around six months ago, Hazel and Cora had been kidnapped and abandoned in a hollow, titanic oak tree right when Melanie had figured out the truth about her father. Melanie had turned to her friends for support, but they were gone. It had all happened so quickly, Hazel and Cora didn't even have time to react. A lady with sweeping chestnut hair and thin brows in a hooded navy cloak had stealthily swooped them into her arms and dashed off into the sky. It should've taken a couple hours to arrive where they did, but the lady had jumped through the air and arrived at the oak tree in less than a second. It was impossible, but living in the forest helped the two girls know that nothing was impossible in The Trenside Thicket. The lady had laid them gingerly on the floor, not even gagging them with cloth or even binding their wrists. She just grabbed Cora's sword, Excalibur and ran off. The two girls had tried everything to escape but had no luck. They were just stuck in a tree, with no doors. At first, they were a mess of worry. But as the days went by, food would mysteriously appear with two glasses of water. Nothing bad had happened and their panic had eased. Hazel had spent most of her time worrying about Melanie, pondering if she was okay and what had happened in the time that they had been gone. Cora racked her brain for strategies to get out of the tree without a sword, which was hard for her because she relied on swords for almost everything. But the both girls each shared one worry: Would Melanie think that they had left her?

When "the ritual" echoed through the forest once again, the two girls' faces brightened with new hope. Melanie must have a plan to get them out, she must still have faith in them! But Melanie wouldn't just play "the ritual" over and over again for no reason. So why was she?

"Cora!" Hazel exclaimed, "What if she's using "the ritual" as a code?"

Cora scratched her head, thinking.

"Well, let's first remember what it means," she said.

Hazel raised her brows.

"Really," Cora huffed. "Do I need to explain everything?

The Tap equals her bond. Roar equals mine, and Clap equals yours. So maybe it has to do with our Bonds?"

Hazel sat down, head whirring with possibilities.

"Maybe..." she drawled, dubious. But then, another sound came from far away:

CLAP. CLAP. CLAP. CLAP. CLAP. CLAP.

"It's clapping! That's my bond!" Hazel whispered. Hazel sorted through the thoughts in her head until she looked down at her shining locket. She remembered what Merlin had said:

"This locket will let you see into two people's hearts. Put the golden heart above the person's and you will hear all of their thoughts and wishes. And if you really want to, you can grant one of them. You can grant anyones. But beware, you can only use it twice."

Hazel's eyes widened in understanding. She pressed her lips into a smile. Melanie was quite the intelligent friend. How had she not seen it before?

"Cora," she exclaimed, her voice a hushed but excited whisper. "She wants me to use my locket."

Seconds later, Hazel was unlatching her locket. Cora took in a breath, glancing at her friend nervously.

"You can do it," she said, exhaling painfully. Hazel nodded while swallowing. She pressed the golden heart to her chest. Merlin had said she would be able to hear anyones thoughts and wishes. He had also said that, if she wishes, she could grant one of them. Millions of tiny whispers crowded Hazel's thoughts. She was hearing all of her wishes. Flurries of words pounded at her brain. Hazel groaned, head aching. Cora gripped her hand. Hazel found it assuring until she saw that her friend's hand was painted with cold sweat. Hazel forced herself to make her wish clearer.

"I wish to bring Cora and I to Melanie." The voice echoed loudly for a moment but was then overlapped by her screaming thoughts.

"I WISH TO BRING CORA AND I TO MELANIE!" she screeched, turning a bit hysterical.

Cora let go of her hand, surprised and scared. The world started turning upside down, twirling and spinning. Cora's face quickly became a pale shade of green. Hazel gripped her friend. They both spiraled into the air until they could smell fresh dew and wet grass. They opened their eyes. In front of them—was Melanie, eyes glistening with tears of shocked relief.

Chapter 27
The Serpent With No Tail

Melanie's sagging heart straightened to its full height. Her eyes brimmed with happiness and she jumped into her friend's open arms. They were safe! They were here!

Her friend's exploded into mixed emotions. "Tell us everything!" gasped Cora.

And so she did. She started right off when they disappeared, when she had fallen into The Hudson River, met Natalie, been framed for the destruction of Riverhaven, saved the vanishing town, and so on until she finished in her friends arms again. Hazel was ogling her, eyes shining with disbelief but the feeling that she knew Melanie was telling the truth. Cora was gaping at Briarrides, reaching out to touch him but then thinking better of it. Briarrides tried to smile. In the view of Cora, it looked like a scowl and puff of smoke and she scurried back to her friends. Melanie chuckled through tears. She had her friends back!

After their moment of relief, Hazel and Cora explained the kidnapping by a hooded lady in the navy. Melanie's eyes widened but she didn't say anything. Natalie had a dark navy cloak. They then explained that they were imprisoned in a hollow, huge oak tree. It was Natalie's turn to be surprised, but nobody noticed.

"Oh, um I nearly forgot..." said Melanie, swallowing the small frog in her throat, "Cora, Hazel, this is Natalie... my f-foster... mother." Saying the words didn't sound right anymore. Melanie couldn't tell her friends about Natalie now, she would have to later.

"Nice to meet you!" said Cora.

"I bet you're great!" chimed Hazel. Melanie cringed at the comment and Natalie laughed. Melanie hated how happy Natalie looked, how good at acting she was.

"I think that before we go to the Woods Master, we should ask something or someone that knows him," said Melanie.

"Isn't that pretty risky?" asked Hazel.

Melanie pursed her lips. She hadn't thought of that.

"Um... I... well."

Before she could think of an answer, Natalie intervened. "I think it's a great idea!" she said.

Melanie suddenly felt sick but Cora answered before she could:

"Alright then, let's do it! But... how?"

A hiss pierced at Melanie's ear. She jumped back.

"Did anyone else hear tha—?" she began.

But by the pale looks on their faces, they had. A cobra's head appeared above Cora's and Melanie screamed. The cobra swept by her and faced the crowd, yellow teeth gleaming. The snake had army green scales that covered his whole body, a circular head and gleaming black eyes, and a blood-red forked tongue. The only strange part about him was that he was hovering mid-air and...

"H-Has no t-tail!" stuttered Melanie, gripping her hands for them to stop shaking.

"Yessss" hissed the snake, head cocking to the side. "I am the tailless sssnake," he said, voice raspy and crisp. He emphasized certain letters like they were stronger than others.

"I heard your wissh," he said the last word in a shrillier voice, smiling eveily at Melanie.

Natalie and Sapphire had cowered back, leaving a shell-shocked Cora and sheet white Hazel trying to reach out to Melanie, who was cornered by the cobra.

"I can ssenssse magic in you," he said slithering closer through the air. "I sssensse a double creation."

A double creation? Melanie thought that the snake had lost his mind. "Um. sorry Mr. Snake," said Melanie hastily, "I uh, have no... double creation."

"Ah," said the snake, smiling jeeringly, "I ssee Merlin hasss lied again. Even to the girl who'll sssave him one day."

Melanie teetered back, shocked. He's lying, she thought. He has to be lying. Melanie looked at Natalie for support but she was looking down at her shoes, throat bobbing. What was going on?

"Merlin hassss a tendency to lie and then reveal the truth too late," the snake jeered. "I asssume he didn't tell you about other thingsss. Like a … Book?" the snake chaffed.

Melanie choked on her spit. Behind the snake, Natalie's jaw dropped. So did Hazel's, Cora's and Sapphire's. They knew what "the book" was. The Woods Master's hoarse voice ripped through her thoughts:

"Melanie, if you'd like to know why it's Riverhaven I seek to destroy, then you should go to Merlin and ask him for: The Book. He's been hiding something from you."

What *was* Merlin hiding from her?

"Merlin hasssn't told you much about yoursssself. You may want to talk to him before you depart to the Woodss Massster."

"But how? And what are you doing here?"

"I undersssstand why the Woodss Massster thinksss you aren't sssso bright. I'll make sure to mention your location. It will sssserve ussss. Maybe after all this my disappearing jewels and money will come back."

In a flash, the cobra disappeared. Hazel and Cora ran to her, hurling questions and words. But Melanie wasn't looking at them. She was looking at Natalie, who was sitting with hunched shoulders, refusing to meet her eyes, hiding something. Melanie knew the truth now, even if she tried to run from it. Natalie was the spy.

Chapter 28
The Animal Guardian

Melanie was raging in anger. Merlin lied. Natalie lied. What was the truth? She was going to figure it out... Now. But Sapphire was still recovering from the hard landing and Briarrides was tired. And they had two more companions on their quest now. Melanie thought about walking to Merlin's. No, too long. She thought about leaving Natalie behind. No, to mean. Her mind finally settled on one option: she was going to try and summon another animal to help her and her friends —and Natalie— fly to Merlin's. She concentrated on her love of animals. She concentrated on how much she needed help.

"Please," she whispered, as quiet as a mouse, "We need a ride."

A beam of light erupted below her and Melanie staggered back. Hazel and Cora looked at Melanie, awed. But instead of an animal, a black haired lady appeared. Her hair was put in a long, winding ponytail, a helmet with two tusks blocking out the front. She had tanned skin and eyebrows that looked like two streaks of thin paint with frecklesthat painted her nose. She was wearing a sweeping beige gown. In other words: absolutely gorgeous .

"I am The Animal Guardian," she declared, her voice loud and clear.

Melanie had met many people in the Thicket but this person was the only one that didn't look greedy or mischievous. She just looked calm and composed.

"I have come to help Miss McGee."

Melanie gawked at her.

"Oh my goodness, Melanie!" whispered Cora excitedly.

"You just summoned The Animal Guardian!" squeaked Hazel, breathless and stupefied, eyes shining like millions of stars. Hazel swept a magnificent bow so low to the ground her hair touched it.

"I-it's an honor."

Cora and Natalie swept their own bows so Melanie tried as well, though hers was wobbly and her neck hurt so she staggered to the side .

The Guardian was illuminated by a soft gold glow that shifted in the direction that she moved.

"I heard a double creation's wish to know the truth. I see big power and kindness in you, Melanie. I haven't seen a bond like yours in some time. Only double creations have that bond, like you... and I."

Melanie beamed at her, not exactly knowing why.

"Uh." she said, "Your Highness? Um... what's a double bond?"

"That isn't for me to tell you, Melanie," she said.

Melanie pushed down her anger. Why did everyone tell her that? Even Hazel and Cora knew what the lady was talking about. Why couldn't she?

"Your friends haven't told you because they can't," she said, reading her thoughts, "It is your quest, so you must figure it out. The Book will tell you."

Melanie's anger was replaced with deep eagerness to figure out what The Book was. For a reason Melanie couldn't identify, her heart lifted out of its limp mess of sorrow.

"Thank you, Animal Guardian," Melanie breathed.

"Please," she said, "Call me Maeve, I guard the mythical animals and seek out loving souls. Goodbye, Melanie."

Melanie felt her feet lift from the ground and soar into the air. But, unlike all the other times she flew, she didn't feel afraid of heights. She closed her eyes and soared higher and higher until she felt herself fall to grass beside Cora, Hazel, Natalie, Briarrides, and Sapphire; right next to Merlin's house.

Chapter 29
The Spy or The Innocent?

Hazel, Cora and Melanie had already entered the Merlin's house, charging in at the drifting smell of stackaberry soup. Natalie had stayed behind for a moment. As Melanie tumbled into the house, Natalie noticed a crumpled piece of paper fall to the floor and picked it up, uncrumpling the paper and peering at the cursive writing that began with: *Dearest Melanie.* Natalie scanned the page with wide eyes. What was this? All the worries about Melanie's strange attitude after not finding the feather clicked into place. Melanie had gone, found the note instead of the feather, and was now believing that she was a spy for The Woods Master. Natalie had clung onto the hope that Walter McGee was captured, but she knew the truth now, Walter had sided with The Woods Master ... And he was about to lure Melanie to him.

While Melanie had walked into the apartment she had hurriedly flurried out what the letter had said from her father to Cora and Hazel. They each shared their opinions:

"Are you sure, Melanie? Natalie seems so nice!" said

Hazel.

"Yeah, maybe your father made a mistake," chimed Cora.

"No," said Melanie sharply, "I'll show you the letter myself." Melanie reached into her pocket for the note but only grabbed air. A bone-chilling dread hit her hard. Where was the note? Did Natalie... find it? Melanie didn't have time to speak. Out of nowhere, a hologram of Walter's face, flickering and glitching came into view. Melanie could see that behind him, there were cell bars and an empty, cement-covered room, polished and clean.

"Father?" Melanie breathed, wondering how he had casted the projection. "Is that you?"

Walter nodded, turning his head nervously around every other second.

"We don't have much time, Melanie. Have you gotten as far away from Natalie as possible? Have you severed contact?" Melanie glanced down, her face feeling hot. Melanie, though as much as she tried to ignore it, still loved her foster mother and couldn't imagine her as a spy. Walter frowned.

"Melanie, you need to get away from her. She's dangerous and is feeding The Woods Master information! Where are you?" He asked, eyes narrowing at the sight of Cora and Hazel. "And... weren't those the two girls who abandoned you?"

Melanie shook her head.

"They were kidnapped by a lady in a navy cloak," said Melanie, glancing back at the door where Natalie seemed to be picking something off from the ground.

"Natalie wears navy!" Said Walter, eyes slashing through Melanie in panic.

"You know Natalie?" asked Melanie curiously. Walter's face darkened.

"From high school," he said bitterly, "always tried to mess up my good grades." Melanie nodded but felt no pity for her dad. She still liked Natalie, no matter how many times her dad told her she was evil. The screen blurred and Walter's voice turned fuzzy.

"Melanie, where are you? You need to come quick."

"I'm in Merlin's house," said Melanie, raising her voice so her flickering father could hear her, "I'm finally going to get the answers I wanted. I'm going to read "The Book."" Melanie hadn't expected for her father to know what "The Book" was but she stood corrected. Walter's eyes flared.

"No! Melanie, do not read that book under any circumstances," he quipped, "It's dangerous."

Melanie ignored him.

"Melanie!" growled Cora urgently, "you're making a

racket. Natalie can hear you."

"Do not read it Melanie," roared Walter. Melanie smiled apologetically.

"I'm sorry, father," she said, hands raised, "I need to know." Walter screamed an answer but Melanie slashed through his glitching reflection with her hand.

"I'm sorry, father," she said again, walking deeper into the apartment with Hazel and Cora at her side. It was time to get answers.

Chapter 30
The Story

Merlin's apartment smelled like stackaberry soup. Melanie's mouth watered. Stackaberry soup, Merlin's signature dish, had been served to Melanie when she had met the wizard and her two friends for the first time. She had craved that taste many times at home and now just wanted to chug down all of what Merlin owned. A deep humming came from the kitchen. Melanie and the two girls rushed in, stomach's rumbling. Natalie stayed back with Sapphire. Since Briarride had to stay outside, Natalie offered to watch over him. Melanie felt uncomfortable leaving the spy with her animal friends but concluded that, if she attacked them, they could fend for themselves.

Melanie, Hazel, and Cora came in to find Merlin with three bowls of soup.

"Hazel, Cora, Melanie, what a surprise," he said, urging them to slip down his food. They glared at him, saying silently to use his sarcasm later. He watched them eat in silence.

"Melanie," he said gently, once they had finished their soup, "I know that you have many questions and that you must be pretty upset with me for not telling the truth. And I know that you're probably wondering: What's The Book? What did everyone mean by double creation? What's the deal with Natalie? And Hazel and Cora's kidnapper? You also have other questions about the future, I know. Why are you going to save me? When? I can only answer the questions about the past. All of the answers are in a book, Melanie. One that I have been hiding from you since you figured out the truth of your father. But I can't hide it from you anymore." He handed Melanie a small, leather book and nodded at her to read it. This was the moment when all of her confusion would be answered! But why did she feel that churning dread in her stomach then? Was she afraid of the truth? Was she afraid of what she would figure out? She opened the book and took in a breath:

The Birth of Riverhaven

Unknown Author (but credit is sometimes given to the woods pen)

Once upon a time, it began. Melanie groaned. She had always despised stories that started that way, claiming that there was no thrill to it. Merlin glared at her and she continued.

Once upon a time, there was a world without magic. There were no fairy tales and no one believed in legends or myths.

Deep down in the pits of the earth, a creature who is now known as The Realm Jumper created Riverhaven. She wanted a town where all children's dreams could live. She extracted a piece of her soul and turned it into Riverhaven, making her wish come true. But for every wish, you need to pay a price. The lady was forever cursed. She could go from one place to another in an instant, yes, but the curse set a great burden on her family. Anyone who tried to fall in love in her family would be taken away forever. Only her and her sister stayed alive. Along with the town, two more things came with it: Riverhaven was placed on the other side of The Trenside Thicket and a caretaker who went by The Woods Master who had to watch over the animals and protect them from any dangers.

For a couple centuries (he was immortal) everything worked out. People would come and visit and the man that wished for Riverhaven grew up and had a child, but stayed immortal. But then, The Woods Master grew careless. He liked his job, yes. The town respected him like a king and they gave him all the luxuries he wished for. But with the luxuries came great responsibility. At the time, the townsfolk and mythical creatures weren't at war. In fact, they were the best of friends. But the caretaker of the town, The Woods Master, was the one that was responsible to keep the balance so that the townsfolk and the creatures

could get along. When small arguments between both species started to break out, Riverhaven started questioning The Woods Master's ability to be their caretaker. When he was ordered out of the town, he sent splashes of black paint to bind up anyone, animal or human, that questioned him. Black paint doesn't seem like much but The Woods Master was a double creation. And double creations can have remarkable power. He had turned the black droplets into spears of black steel and, if he wished, The Woods Master could make them even deadlier: like poisoned tips, or flexible eel-like droplets that could morph into objects. For a long time, Riverhaven lived in fear. But while that fear was building, the war that would later go on for 200 years, started. Since The Woods Master had slowly started abandoning his duties as caretaker and using it to watch the citizens and animals cower in fear as he walked by, the war began. Somewhere around the middle of the war, The Woods Master had been exiled, banished to live in the deadly Trenside Thicket forever. Every time The Woods Master tried to enter Riverhaven, it rebounded back at him and shot him into the forest like a horse bucking off its passenger. No one had ever heard of him since, though rumor had spread that he had been plotting to get his revenge on the town.

A couple years later in New York City, The Realm Jumper's sister was trying to lead a normal life. Being a

double creation herself, The Realm Jumper's sister was always afraid of her bond. She didn't want to end up with a bond that was harmful: like revenge or greed. So she spent her whole life trying to make the magic inside her disappear. But it wasn't long until she realized her bond, mostly by mistake. Even though The Realm Jumper's sister tried to isolate herself from everything, she still visited the zoo everyday, comforted by the animals. One day, the 14th of May, she peered at a panda that looked so lonely and whispered:

"Dear panda, I hope you're alright." She didn't expect a response but, startlerly, she heard a small, fresh whisper say:

"I'm quite alright, don't worry about me. I see you figured out what your bond is." The Realm Jumper's sister's bond was an extremely rare one: she could hear animal's thoughts and wishes, she could befriend any animal. Once she had figured her bond out, The Realm Jumper's sister found it impossible to hide herself from the rest of the world. Forgetting about the curse that was placed on her family, she made friends and eventually fell in love with a man named Walter Bandswith McGee. He was a man who was never allowed to go to Riverhaven so, as all of you must know, he disobeyed his parents and went, *took the Bird of Steel's feather and was later defeated by his daughter.*

That was around the time the war was ending . Walter and The Realm Jumper's sister got married and had a child: Melanie McGee. But The Realm Jumper's sister had forgotten about the curse and soon, the world got ready to take her away. But the universe took pity on her and saw an amazing bond and love for animals. So instead of letting The Realm Jumper's sister die, they gave her another job in exchange for her death. Since Riverhaven didn't have a caretaker anymore, they made her immortal and turned her into Riverhaven's new caretaker for all eternity. Soon after, Walter figured out the truth about his wife and The Realm Jumper's sister couldn't stay with her family. She was forced to live in Riverhaven, even though she begged to have her family come with her. Over time, she tried and tried to stay in touch with her husband but he started to turn bitter and clipped, thinking that his wife enjoyed the job and preferred it over her family. He then figured out his bond: revenge. Walter McGee spent the rest of his life making sure no one believed in Riverhaven. Once he had done that, he dedicated his work to getting his revenge on The Realm Jumper's sister. The Realm Jumper's sister was heartbroken when she realized what Walter was doing. She did her job well, but she once again hid herself from everyone as much as possible. But it was hard doing that knowing that her daughter was in the Woods trying to save

her father who she kept thinking was good. *So after a long time, she couldn't keep hidden. When Melanie McGee was put into foster care, she adopted her daughter but not telling Melanie that she is her actual mother. She was waiting for the right moment to reveal to her daughter who she truly was.*

A note on The Realm Jumper

The Realm Jumper is one of the few Double Creations who can teleport to other places in less than a second. *It has been told that the Realm Jumper was working for The Woods Master for money if you handed in to him one of the below:*

Melanie McGee

Hazel Perkins

Cora Jackson

Natalie McGee

Merlin

The Realm Jumper handed in Cora Smith and Hazel Perkins and got 456,000 woods coins. The Realm Jumper isn't known to work for evil but she was robbed and needed the money. **Fun fact: The Realm Jumper has no bond anymore due to the horrible impact of her granting Walter' wish.**

A note on Walter McGee and The Woods Master

Currently, it has been known that Walter McGee has been trying to get his revenge on Natalie and Riverhaven. But he isn't the only one. The Woods Master is also holding a grudge against the young (but not so young, technically) woman, because she had replaced him after all. Rumor says that the two have been plotting together for their revenge.

A note on Double Creations

Double creations are rare species of humans. They are the children of a mother and father who are both created or become later in their life from the deepest pits of magic. It usually results in the child having extremely powerful bonds and their story broadcasted through the woods from the Woods Pen. Double Creations are also known to commonly inherit some of the bonds of either their mother or father.

*Everything that is in italic, indicates that those were newer notes added into the book after it was written and published

Chapter 31
With Answers Comes More Questions

Melanie tried to find a word to describe how she was feeling. She couldn't. The ability to speak was ripped out of her and she just sat on the chair, looking down at the book and avoiding eye contact with the rest of the group. For the first time in her life, Melanie had no lost thoughts or defensive words to save her. Instead, she turned away from everyone and thought:

I'm a double creation. Natalie is the Realm Jumper's sister. Natalie is my mother! Natalie is my mother! She exclaimed in her head again, a sizzling feeling tickling her tongue. But then the last thought came:

"Is father working with The Woods Master? It says he wants revenge on Natalie, not Riverhaven. This—"

"We know, Melanie," said Hazel softly.

"We still need to figure that part out," soothed Cora gently.

"Melanie, you are a double creation which most likely means your story will be broadcasted through the woods," said Merlin. Melanie didn't respond. She wasn't ready to speak to him yet. And she didn't want to admit that she had no clue about what he was talking about. "There is this thing called the Woods Pen. If the Woods Pen senses a good ending for a story, they write about it and make it into fairy tales and broadcast it to the woods. Hazel has been broadcasted and so has Cora. And by the looks of it, your story has started to be written as well." Merlin handed her a thick book with a background that looked like paint and a feather in the middle. Above it, slimy black paint bullets slashed across the page. That was the cover. It read:

The Tale of Melanie McGee

Melanie froze like a statue. She gaped at Merlin in disbelief but he showed no sign of this being a fake.

"The Woods Pen is writing about me?" she breathed. "The whole world will see this soon." Merlin shook his head.

"Only the woods, for now. People like Cinderella and Peter Pan became so famous throughout the woods that the pen sent it to the rest of the world and earned a profit from it." Melanie skimmed through the pages and gasped. It had been writing about her since before she came to Riverhaven! She flicked through more pages: Her driving to Riverhaven, meeting "Mr. Bandswith," befriending Sapphire, seeing Merlin and her friends, finding the feather, chased into the woods by police, etc, etc; until she got to the last page where the book was painting a picture of her gawking at the book itself in a flurry of colored ink. Beneath the image, it said:

Melanie would face heartbreak, sacrifice, and something worse than death today; but in which order?

Melanie swiveled to Merlin, horror masking her face. Something worse than death?

"It could just mean that you had to sacrifice a shoe or something," said Cora weakly.

"Yeah, or break a paper heart in two..." trailed Hazel with nervous pursed lips.

Melanie felt herself quiver from all parts of her body. But instead of feeling depressed or weak, all she felt was raw anger at everything. Before she could stop herself, Melanie was raging at her friends:

"I'm thirteen years old, thirteen years old! And I'm worrying about surviving. I don't care if you guys have lived here your whole life, it's not normal! I don't know what fairy tales were written about you or if your mom is Snow White... this is absurd. And Merlin," she growled, charging at the bearded man, "I've had so many questions and you know that! But you don't answer me until I finish suffering through all the pain that everyone has caused me and let me figure it all out from a book! A book!" Melanie tried to stop but she had more to say.

Merlin had blinked back calmly but Hazel and Cora

were desperately trying to talk to her.

"Melanie..." breathed Hazel, eyes flooding with tears.

"No!" Melanie screamed. At that moment, Natalie came running in.

"Melanie. What's—?" she began.

"And you," growled Melanie, her face darkening to a dark muddy pool of anger, "You wait 'till after I think you're a spy, after I think I have no family left, to let me know that you're MY MOTHER?!" Natalie sagged and gave Melanie a sad look.

"Melanie..."

Melanie was now balling up her fists and roaring at her limp crowd. She glared at each one of them separately and bit her lip until she could taste blood. Then, she stormed out of the room, making sure that her feet echoed loudly off of the wood. The last thing that Melanie heard was the thumping of the Woods Pen's words:

Melanie would face heartbreak, sacrifice, and something worse than death today; but in which order?

Chapter 32
Gimgot and Gotgim

Melanie sprinted into the woods, not particularly going anywhere. Her anger subsided and she clenched her fists in frustration. I can't do this anymore, she thought. I need Merlin, Hazel and Cora to help me. Thinking of her two best friends and the way she had treated them back at Merlin's made her want to sit down and so . Shame colored her anger-flushed cheeks until she decided that she had to go back and apologize. In reality, everyone had to apologize for everything but she was too exhausted to think straight. When Melanie turned, though, she found a bridge over a fast flowing stream that was surely not there before. She braced herself for the worst. In the woods, if anything appeared out of nowhere, it was never a good sign.

Hesitantly, Melanie put one foot onto the bridge. Two soot-covered identical trolls appeared from beneath her. She jumped back. The two trolls had identical red trousers and rags for shirts. They had messy, greasy brown hair that looked black by the amount of ash covering their scalp. They grinned, revealing yellow teeth. Melanie smiled nervously back. But these trolls looked different, they didn't have that sneer that most of the villains did. They just looked confused.

"Me Gotgim!" said the first troll.

"Gimgot!" roared the second troll happily. Melanie couldn't help but snicker.

"Um... excuse me... Gotgim and Gimgot, could I please pass?" she asked politely.

"No passing Gotgim's bridge," said the troll, crossing his arms and pouting stubbornly.

"No! No passing *Gimgot's* bridge," said the other.

"Gotgim's bridge!" said Gotgim narrowing his eyes at his twin.

"This is Gimgot's bridge!" roared the other. Melanie sighed. This was going to take a long time.

"Is there anything I can give you in exchange for my passage?" asked Melanie, trying to keep the impatience out of her voice. The two trolls smiled greedily.

"Treasure!" roared Gotgim. Gimgot glared at his twin.

"Gimgot says: Treasure!"

The two trolls raised their pudgy fists at each other. Melanie intervened before the fight could break out:

"I don't have any treasure," she said.

The trolls looked down at the golden bracelet on her

wrist. Melanie shook her head.

Around a year and a half ago, Merlin had made that bracelet and said that whenever she was in danger, she could tap it three times and something "magical" would save her. He had also said that she would know when to use it. Now didn't seem like the right time and she wasn't going to give it up to two trolls that argued over everything.

"Gimgot likes treasure!" simpered Gimgot.

"No," pouted Gotgim, "*Gotgim* likes treasure!"

"I can't give you that," replied Melanie, her impatience increasing by the second. She had to get back to Hazel and Cora.

Gimgot narrowed his eyes.

"Give Gimgot treasure!" he said, walking closer to Melanie and trying to snatch her bracelet.

"Give *Gotgim* treasure!" said Gotgim murderously. Melanie looked for a hole to bury herself in. Melanie had had enough.

"AGHHHH!" She roared. Out of nowhere, Briarrides appeared and spewed flames at the two trolls. Melanie stopped her impatient screaming.

"No!" she said. Melanie was angry at these trolls, yes, but she hadn't intended to get them roasted and skewered by a dragon. Melanie sprinted towards the two trolls, hurled the two trolls to the ground and grabbed them by the wrists, flinging herself and the two onto the other side of the bridge. Briarrides let out an angry puff.

"Who you" asked Gotgim.

"I'm Melanie," she answered, panting.

"Mel save Gotgim life!" replied Gotgim giddily.

"Mal save Gimgot life!" roared Gimgot coldly to his twin.

"Her name is Mel!" snapped Gotgim.

"Mal!" roared Gimgot.

"Mel!"

"Mal!"

"Moo!"

The trolls continued their battle of words so vigorously, they didn't notice the girl who they were arguing about scampering away from the burnt remains of their bridge.

Chapter 33
Ashley Returns

Natalie never felt so sick in her life. She knew it had been wrong to let her daughter suffer like how she did. She knew that Melanie would eventually figure out.

"This is horrible," whispered Natalie.

Natalie, of course, knew that but saying it out loud made the reality real. Where was Melanie?

After her daughter had run out of the house, the crew searched inside and out for her. They found nothing? Was Melanie alright? Was she even alive? Her daughter would come eventually, she thought urgently. Of course she will. But the more she thought about it, the more doubts clouded her thoughts. The sound of thumps on the floor, brought Natalie back to the present.

"Melanie?" she asked hopefully. A man with white hair and beard in a navy cloak swooped in.

"Oh," Natalie said, "It's you."

"You don't need to sound so disappointed," laughed Merlin.

Natalie sighed and went back to her thoughts. Merlin didn't leave.

"What is it, Merlin?" asked Natalie.

"Melanie still holds hope that your husband isn't siding with The Woods Master. Anyone who ignores the truth and clings onto a love that isn't there anymore is a dangerous role in the story, Natalie. You know that way too well." Natalie nodded, but wasn't listening. "Natalie, we don't have much time before The Woods Master and Walter will carry through their plan." Natalie was awake now, suddenly listening.

"We need to find Melanie now," said Natalie, Merlin's hidden proposal revealing itself to her. Luckily, they didn't need to go look for her. Melanie came crashing into the room, gripping her bracelet like she had nearly lost it.

"What happened?" asked Natalie, worried.

"That's not important right now," panted Melanie. "I'm sorry, really. I didn't mean what I said. I was just—"

"We understand," said Natalie hastily, "This was our fault, not yours." Melanie nodded and Merlin continued off of where Natalie had started.

"Melanie, we need to go. Now."

Hazel and Cora came rushing in, a sword (though not Excalibur) strapped to Cora's waist. They smiled at Melanie serenely, telling her that they had heard the conversation and forgave her. For a moment, Melanie smiled back and that soothing warmth blossomed in her chest. Then she saw Merlin's expression.

"Right, let's go!"

The troop of girls charged out the door, Cora roaring a battle cry, Natalie beside them, and Sapphire rushing in to join. But Merlin hadn't budged.

"Merlin...!?"

He didn't answer. The wizard's eyes were glassy and he was gazing off into the distance, rain slowly starting to pour.

"Merlin! We need to go!"

The wizard crumpled. Natalie gasped and shut the door behind her, rain thumping louder now. Melanie glanced at Hazel, who was a medical expert, but Hazel just shrugged nervously.

Cora sprinted to Melanie, eyes wide.

"Do something!" she yelled over the rain, even though they were inside the house.

Melanie glared back. "Just because this is my story doesn't mean I always know what to do," squawked Melanie nervously. Natalie was holding Merlin gently by his arms, laying him down on a couch. The wizard's breaths were shallow and raspy. Melanie's chest was rising up and down, up and down, sweat pouring from different directions.

Melanie's voice was choked. In one second, Merlin had gone from a leader to an unconscious man.

"Will he-will he be alright?" cried Melanie, throat painfully clogged and eyes blurring with unwashed, salty tears.

Natalie nodded, but everyone knew that no one could know for sure. Melanie reached out for Merlin's hand and found it bony, a bright blue vein showing itself. Melanie trembled. No matter how many times she became impatient with the wizard's mysterious answers of: you'll see and you'll know later, Merlin was family. Just like Natalie.

When you say that Hazel is an exceptional doctor, maybe even better than an adult, that is no exaggeration. Hazel rushed to Merlin's side and inspected him.

Merlin's breathing was slowing down and little black squiggles were starting to paint his face.

"What's wrong with him?" exclaimed Cora.

Merlin's face was a sickly pale and his lips were cracked, any color that was on them faded into a sickening blue color.

"He needs to get to a hospital!" she said. Natalie rushed to the phone and dialed 911. In a couple of minutes, a Woods Ambulance was hauling Merlin into the car. Before he departed, Merlin slowly opened his eyes and rasped:

"Go! The Woods Master is waiting..."

***

Melanie was flying on Briarrides in the air but felt no fear of heights like how she usually did. She just felt hollow emptiness in her stomach scraping away at more insides. While Natalie was in a hushed conversation with Cora, Hazel was sitting tensely in her seat, looking back at Melanie nervously.

"You know what happened to Merlin, don't you?" asked Melanie sourly.

"What," gasped Hazel, "Of course not!"

But Melanie knew that Hazel was lying. Sapphire was treading air behind her as she magically galloped towards Melanie in the air, nuzzling her companion like she knew what Melanie was going through. Melanie shoved it off forcefully. In the distance, an inky black cloud crept over the horizon, obscuring part of the sun and starting to consume the rest of it. The hollowness in Melanie's stomach deadened. A shiny black bullet was slithering towards her. Once it had come close enough, Melanie slashed at it with her hand, nearly toppling over Briarrides but regaining balance, then stomping the bullet to a pulp on Briarrides's tough helmet of

skin. Melanie wiped it off of Briarrides with her hand. It was...
paint.

Just a couple days ago, Melanie had faced the Woods
Master and seen the ripply sheen of slithering black paint
bullets covering his body like a suit. Melanie hadn't cared
much about it at the time (trying to survive and all.) But after
reading the book about the birth of Riverhaven, she realized
that this paint wasn't just the villain's specialty, but the
stuff he had used to postpone his exile by putting the town
in a state of fear, until they overcame it and banished him
permanently from the town.

"We must be close to The Woods Master," said Melanie.

Natalie and Cora stopped their conversation and
looked into the distance.

"What makes you say that?" asked Natalie.

"One of his paint minions just got beaten up by my
foot," said Melanie proudly, beaming back at her mother.
All of her anger had disappeared when Merlin had fallen,
like nothing had ever happened between the mother and
daughter.

Hazel snickered, followed by Cora, then Natalie, and
eventually Melanie herself.

The snickering stopped when Briardes looked down
and belched fire, indicating something was below. Melanie

squinted her eyes. A wave of bright orange hair, slightly curled and frizzy, but amazingly gorgeous flurried through the trees. Melanie recognized that hair.

"Lower us!" demanded Melanie, using her eyes to chase the red-headed girl. What was Ashley doing in the forest? Melanie swiveled to Hazel and Cora who both had the same wide-eyed, open-mouthed expressions as her.

Briarrides thumped to the muddy forest floor. The trio of friends rushed off into the forest. Briarrides glared at Melanie in a way that said *oh, don't mind me, I'll just sit here patiently and wait an hour for you. No need to thank me for the ride.* Sapphire looked at Briarides in a warning that looked like *please be polite or I'll poke you in the eye with my horn.* Briarides kept his thoughts to himself after that.

"Ashley!" Said Cora.

"Wait!" screeched Hazel.

"Ashley!!" said Melanie, louder than her two friends. The girl didn't stop running. Ashley was now sprinting through the forest, slashing at trees and crumpling flowers as she dashed by. Melanie screamed louder.

"ASHLEY!" she bellowed.

Ashley... stopped. It may have been how urgent Melanie sounded, or the pain in her legs demanding her to stop running, or the way Melanie looked at her like she was her only hope. Whatever it was, Ashley stopped running and let the three girls jog up to her, dabbing at sweat and stretching their legs.

"What are you doing here?" accused Ashley. Melanie folded her arms, giving her a cold look.

"We are wondering the same for you." she snipped. Ashley fell silent. For a long moment, no one spoke and a building tension separated the girls. Then, like a balloon who had just exploded, Ashley wailed:

"It's Oliveeeer!" Cora and Hazel both stiffened. Melanie looked at them. The name sounded familiar, vaguely. Melanie was immediately brought to the moment when she had met Cora, Hazl, and Ashley. But she had also met a grumpy black-haired boy who seemed to dislike Melanie more than Ashley did.

"Oliver, as in the boy who stormed out of the room the day I met him?" Melanie asked.

Hazel nodded uncomfortably and Cora looked at her fingers and picked at her nails. Her two friends seemed to have a problem with Oliver, thought Melanie. Ashley continued weeping:

"Somebody captured Oliveeeeer! He-he I didn't even noticeee."

Hazel was now blinking randomly while Cora seemed

to be in deep interest of her peeling nailpolish, that's how interesting it seemed. Ashley looked at the trio.

"I-I don't know what to do. But I don't need your help," she added coolly. Cora was now looking at anything but Ashley and Melanie and Hazel was rubbing her palms together, avoiding eye contact from anyone in general. What was wrong with the two? Thought Melanie. And, since she didn't know what else to say, she asked Hazel and Cora just that.

"We've had a... history," mumbled Cora, now devoting herself towards the amazingness of her nails.

"It's... complicated," added Hazel, looking down at her muddy sneakers. Melanie looked at Ashley for more explanation but she just glowered at her like it was all her fault.

"Look," said Melanie, shoving off that horrible feeling of everyone knowing something when she didn't, "Let's set our... differences aside. I bet Oliver is also trapped at the Woods Master's... place like my dad is."

Cora looked at Melanie and said quietly:

"What if we don't want to save Oliver?"

Melanie's astonishment sprung out of her and slathered Cora.

"You-you don't wanna... But why?"

Cora and Hazel both flushed the darkest crimson yet and Melanie eyed them. Ashley was still sobbing.

"It doesn't matter, Melanie." she seethed, "I'm going to find him on my own."

She then flounced around and marched dramatically back into the forest. That was, until she slipped on a rock and landed face first into a pile of mud. She shrieked in disgust.

"Eeeew! What is this?" Hazel and Cora stifled laughs and it clouded out their uncomfortable expressions.

"Ashley, really, we want to help."

Without waiting for Ashley to respond, Melanie gripped her wrist hard and walked her back to Briarrides, Sapphire and Natalie, Hazel and Cora trailing behind her.

Once Ashley had run out of complaining about the spikiness of Briarrides back and how much she wanted a saddle, Ashley, Natalie and Sapphire flew into the air. Melanie had insisted that she stay behind with Cora and Hazel and they would catch up to them on foot. But the real reason that Melanie had done this was to interrogate her friends. She didn't wait another second to start blurting out questions. She started with the one that had always snagged her since they first met.

"What's Ashley's last name? Why does Ashley not want any friends?"

Hazel looked at her as if to say should I answer this? In the end, Hazel replied:

"McMallen is her last name. And to answer your second question: It's her bond. But I'm going to wait for Merlin to tell you that." A wave of fresh tears clung at Melanie when she thought of the wizard but held them back.

"What do you mean? He's in the hospit—"

A flash of purple light appeared and a scraggly looking Merlin trotted up to her, white beard shining through the sunlight. He lay stretched out on the hospital bed looking no healthier than before but clearly mustering up the energy to call. A walking stick was beside him and a tall glass of water. Melanie gaped at Hazel. She smiled back.

"Melanie," he rasped, coughing slightly, "I know that Ashley may seem … But believe me, it isn't her fault. Later on in your journey, you will be faced with something that depends on your friendship. You must become friends and learn to love Ashley. You need to. And this friendship can't be forced. There is something inside Ashley that holds her back from making friends."

"Her bond?" asked Melanie, already knowing the answer.

"Precisely," he said, "But Melanie, keep it in mind, Ashley needs you and you'll need her."

'Pshht," Melanie scoffed.

Merlin slowly faded back into the purple beam of light. As he did so, Melanie pondered what in the world would make her need Ashley McMallen in the next couple of days.

Chapter 34
Ashley's Story

After the encounter with Merlin, Melanie was left a bit frazzled. Something Merlin said still pounded in her head:

"There is something inside Ashley that holds her back from making friends."

It's her bond, thought Melanie. What else would it be?

Melanie's whirring thoughts stopped. Briarrides was already a mile away from the trio. She noticed that Hazel and Cora were already running, so she followed. Why would anyone's bond be so horrible? A bond that makes it hard to make friends. But it's not impossible, she thought, to make friends. So why would Ashley go out of her way to be enemies? More questions slithered into her mind:

Who were Ashley's parents? Who is Oliver? What's Oliver's connection with Ashley? Why does Cora and Hazel hate Oliver so much? Finally, once her legs couldn't bring forth any more energy and she and her friends were at level with Briarrides, she stopped running.

"Briarides!" she said to the sky, "Land please!"

And so the dragon did. Natalie fell to the floor gingerly and swept out a long tent from her satchel.

"We'll be sleeping here tonight," she declared.

Melanie gaped at her in disbelief. "Natalie!" she gasped, "A young boy who's probably on the verge of death and my father are trapped by The Woods Master...That same Woods Master who is probably plotting again on how to destroy Riverhaven and the same man who kept animals hostage and framed me only days ago, but you're thinking about sleeping?!" Melanie fumed with rage until she deflated completely and buckled.

Natalie caught her before she could fall. "You are tired, Melanie. Even if all of this is happening, you can't save them if you fall asleep when they need you."

Melanie crossed her arms. Despite her instinct to keep running, she knew Natalie was right.

"Hazel, Cora, you guys can be in the tent with Melanie. Ashley, you'll be with Sapphire in the other tent. And I'll be in the last one."

Melanie gaped at her mother. "And I thought I was the leader of this quest..."

Ashley grumbled and pointed an accusing finger towards Natalie. "Why do you appoint me with... with ... That?" She glowered at Sapphire.

"At least you're not sleeping on the floor. But if you'd like that, be my guest" snapped Melanie.

Ashley went still. Melanie immediately regretted her words but couldn't muster the courage to apologize.

"Alright then," quipped Natalie with forced cheerfulness and a strained smile, "Let's get into the tents!"

Everyone prepared their tents in an angry silence. Once Ashley had entered her tent and Natalie left to go into hers, Melanie, Cora, and Hazel began their conversation.

"There is something seriously up with Ashley."

Melanie remembered meeting that grumpy boy who now had a name: Oliver. She had looked at Hazel and Cora, silently asking who he was through her eyes. They never had gotten the chance to tell her. Even though her friends were safe now, Melanie's stomach lurched.

"Ashley's life is pretty difficult," said Hazel, choosing her words carefully, "She… uh… has family issues and ignores everyone because of her bond."

"But why?" asked Melanie.

"We don't know," said Cora gravely, "Hazel and I are the closest anyone has ever gotten to be her friends, besides Oliver." Cora's voice instantly turned bitter.

"Could you please tell me why you hate Oliver so much?" pressed Melanie. Hazel stiffened a bit.

"We don't hate him, perce. But we'll tell you that story later."

"Do you think Ashley may be working for The Woods Master? It can be possible..."

"I doubt it," replied Cora sincerely.

"I think we should still check her out," added Hazel. Everyone nodded in agreement. A murmur of assent trickled through the girls.

And so the three friends quietly crept out of their tent and peeked into Ashley's.

"All I see is yellow cotton," murmured Cora.

Hazel stepped on a twig and Cora rebounded to her, looking fierce.

"Now is not the time to move, Hazel," gritted Cora.

A voice amplified through the dark. "Sapphire, I'm leaving the tent. Make sure no one comes in." It was Ashley's slightly high-pitched voice and, by the sound of it, she was applying lipstick onto her rosy red lips.

Hazel ran to the other side of the tent, dragging Cora by the arm. But she couldn't reach out to Melanie and now, Melanie herself was stuck right in front of the door that Ashley was about to leave out of, not even enough time to scamper to her friends. Melanie croaked a strangled "help." Padded footsteps came from inside the tent and Ashley's voice grew louder still.

"And Sapphire, I won't be gone long but there better be nothing misplaced, especially not my diary."

Diary... thought Melanie, she must have written all of her secrets in there! But she wouldn't get to reach the diary if she didn't move. Melanie knew it was silly to be afraid of Ashley figuring out what they were doing but dread still churned like how it had many times before during the journey. Just then, she was yanked to the ground by a red scaly foot. Ashley strode out, her long slightly curly hair in a winding braid and a soft golden dress with small ruffles at the seams.

Melanie gaped in disbelief. Of course: the most practical foot and dress wear for battle: some pretty slippers and a tutu.

"Oh, hello there Briarrides," huffed Ashley in a dignified manner before walking into the forest. Once she was gone, Melanie sighed with relief. She smiled at Briarrides thankfully, realizing he had been the one who had hid her. Hazel and Cora rushed to her, grinning.

"Let's go," they said in unison.

The tent smelled like lavender perfume. The inside was pink with elegant curtains and fake flowers draped everywhere. A long mattress with silk white covers sat in the corner on a plush grey carpet.

"How-how is this possible?" stuttered Melanie. "Our tent looks like a camping disaster and hers is like a room in a mansion."

Cora and Hazel had the same expressions. "How is there a carpet?" mauled Cora, glaring at anything that was pink in the room, "The tent is sitting on grass."

"Who cares about that..." said Hazel, "How did she get the tent like this in five minutes?"

Melanie shrugged and started poking at everything. There were no clothes or suitcases or bags. "She has a diary in here somewhere." said Melanie, still prodding at the mattress.

"Hey!" said Hazel, "I noticed this shiny barret on Ashley's head earlier. Do you think she'd let me keep it?"

Cora glared daggers at her.

"Sorry," murmured Hazel. But when she set it down, the pearl barrett widened until the size of a book and slowly split in half, revealing a black and dusty book with a peeling label that said: Ashley's Diary. The girls gaped, incredulous.

"Ha. That's right, Cora. My comment worked!"

While the rest of the room was pink and full of Ashley, the diary looked old and nothing that the girl would've owned. Hazel opened it cautiously and the three girls peered at the first letter in a swirly cursive script:

Dear Oliver,

I miss you. It's horrible here. It's horrible everywhere. Right now, The Realm Jumper is hiding me beneath a volcano in Hawaii. Don't worry, she enchanted it so no one could get torched by the lava. The Realm Jumper is very kind to me, too kind it seems. I have a feeling you know why. But you don't answer my letters anymore, so I just write them in my diary and pretend that you'll read them one day. The Realm Jumper is sweet. She makes delicious pancakes topped with fluffed fairy dust. I wonder where she gets it? But she said I can't be like this much longer. She said that I can't isolate myself forever like how her sister tried. I ignore her anyway. But I am curious about her sister. Natalie, is the name. Everytime I say it out loud, a warm sensation trickles down my spine. I wonder why... I have dedicated myself to find out everything about my past, even if you don't know it either. Since my bond has made me hide from everyone, that's the only thing I can do to keep myself from being bored. The Realm Jumper said that I don't need to hide. She said that there will be a person, maybe even more, who will love me for who I am. But I haven't found anyone yet, besides you of course.

Melanie stopped reading. How long ago did Ashley write this? She flipped the page to find a different entry.

Oliver,

Where are you??!! I need answers! NOW! But I've searched the Trenside Thicket twice. Twice! And I still can't track your whereabouts. (Though the Woods are quite endless.) I know that you know at least an inkling of my ancestry. I tried not to do what I've forced myself not to but I didn't have much of a choice. I went to Merlin. I know you would be disappointed in me, going back to the man that I love like he's a father again and again. But he is always of great help and you're never there for me, at least not anymore. I need your help. Please come back.

Melanie flipped the page again, desperate for something else. The sentences in the next letter were choppy and seemed to change subject constantly.

Oliver,

I just met these two girls. Hazel and Cora. They were in the Woods together, looking for the original place where The Woods Pen publishes its stories. They seemed so nice. But I've kept my vow to not make friends and I will not break it. When I mentioned I was looking for you, each of them turned ghost-white but wouldn't explain why. I have so many questions but no one will answer them. These girls know Merlin too! So I let them bring me to him, since, though I wouldn't admit it, I was lost. I didn't talk to them though. I wasn't going to be their friend. They brought me to Merlin and… guess what? You were there, your spiky black hair blacker than ever and your shriveled tanned skin tanner than ever before. You will never understand the hurt that I felt. I still write to you, but you never answer. I searched through the whole world to find you and you knew it. But you never came to me. So when I walked through the doors and saw you typing on your phone furiously like you needed to exercise your fingers, the amount of pain in my heart would have crushed Merlin's apartment altogether. You didn't even look at me when I walked in. You just kept typing until you walked out of the room. Hazel and Cora were nicer than ever after that, but it just made me 100% sure I would never ever want to make friends again. Because, even if I don't know why, you betrayed me. And I'm still trying to figure out why I think that.

Melanie whirled to Hazel and Cora. They both looked grim. Melanie knew exactly how much pain Ashley felt. She had been betrayed by someone she loved too. Melanie flipped to see the last letter. But before she did, Melanie went through the image of Oliver. When she had met him, he had ignored everyone. Ashley hadn't looked at him at all, Melanie remembered, but she didn't seem angry or sad if they happened to make eye contact. She would just give him a blank stare like her eyeballs had been gouged out. Oliver was probably 14, a year older than Melanie. His skin, however, that looked wrinkled made him look slightly like an old man, though. I wonder if he got into an accident, thought Melanie. Hazel nudged her and she started reading again:

Dear Oliver,

I shouldn't call you Oliver anymore. I shouldn't even call you a friend. But I still do. My greatest fear was always that, because of my bond being that I'm bad at making friends, if I did end up with a friend, I'd end up ruining that friend's life. I was always worried that if I made a friend, and if they had a fairy tale, I'd somehow ruin it and make it look like I was the villain in the story. But now, I see that the one friend I did let myself make, ruined my tale, even if it was never written by The Woods Pen. But I didn't write this diary entry just to complain. The famous Melanie McGee arrived at Merlin's today. I know that you were there and I still don't understand why. After I saw you at Merlin's you just never spoke. I still don't know why you're doing all of this. So I pretend I'm not hurt. Even though my insides are slowly dying. I don't even need to hear Melanie's voice to know that she is meant to be the leader of her tale. I can see the kindness in her. I know that she was going to fulfill what Merlin predicted. But instead, I did something horrible. I was mean to her and said that I deserved her fate. Melanie, of course, had no idea what I meant. Hazel, Cora, and Melanie all tried to be my friend... and I shot them down. I hate my bond, Oliver! Because of it, I'm forcing myself to be bad and to hide. But I don't want to be bad.

I don't want to hide from everyone else. And now, as The Woods Pen writes Melanie's tale, I've made myself a villain. And I don't know how to turn back. I bet Melanie doesn't want to be friends anymore. I used to hold faith that you'd come to help, but you haven't. So I'm on my own now...

Melanie couldn't believe her eyes. Then, she noticed the stream of tears on her cheek and dabbed at it with her sleeve. Ashley deserved the tale, she thought. Ashley was forcing herself to be out of her spotlight, she's making herself live a painful life. But Melanie saw Cora's face. And it was filled with more than just pain and empathy for Ashley, it was filled with shock. Melanie looked back at the page and saw the words that she hadn't seen before.

Oliver, I don't know what to do. I'm lost. Bye for now...
I love you dad.

Melanie was dumb-struck. The rush of pain that she felt for Ashley was replaced with the worst type of confusion ever: the confusion that said what she had read was impossible. Oliver looked 14. Maybe a bit older, but not old enough to be a father. Not even a relative. This whole time, she had thought that Oliver was Ashley's friend. Even if they were related, (which, thinking about the difference of appearance, was a slim chance) he couldn't be her father.

"But-but"

Melanie didn't have time to look at Cora and Hazel. Because Ashley had walked in and was looking at the girls, mortified and ready to unleash a scream.

Chapter 35
Dangers of Paint

shley's terrified expression turned cold and she started to breathe heavily, clenching her fists until they were as white as her fluffy pillow on her mattress.

"Why are you snooping through my diary?" she choked, trying to sound angry. It only came out defeated. But, when Ashley remembered what her bond was, her eyes flared dangerously and she spat at the girls. But there was a problem. Hazel wasn't there. No one else noticed.

"I've been nothing but nice to you," seethed Ashley. Cora stifled a laugh.

"Oh… yup," drawled Cora sarcastically, "Miss Ashley, the kindest girl in the woods. I'll pay money to see that!"

"Guys…" said Melanie, ignoring the invisible fumes coming from Hazel's and Ashley's ears.

"But you have to go through my stuff!" screeched Ashley in a high-pitched squawk.

"Ashley." Melanie said urgently, panic rising.

"I don't hurt you, I don't do anything bad but ignore

you, for reasons you now know of, because YOU READ MY DIARY!"

"Cora..." breathed Melanie, now gasping for breath as she scanned the room for Hazel.

"Get out!" roared Ashley, strings of her hair coming out of its tight braid and damping to her skull.

"ASHLEY AND CORA!" roared Melanie as loud as she could. Her throat bobbed and she swallowed, tasting the sensation of a dry throat that needed water. The whole tent fell ghostly silent. Melanie now felt like a leader of a quest. She didn't feel like she was only a pawn in a plan she had no control of. Melanie felt powerful. She straightened and said: "Where. Is. Hazel?"

A voice from the corner said, "Ashley, you say we are invading your privacy, yet isn't that a trail of that pink powder you keep in your pocket, trailing into our tent. It looks like we aren't the only people snooping." Hazel emerged from the shadow, eyebrows raised and lips pursed, almost like a smirk.

Melanie slumped in relief. Hazel was just in the corner the whole time, she assured herself. But the relief turned into anger when she realized what Hazel had said.

"You were poking through our tent?" she asked, looking at Ashley, shaking her head, a bit betrayed.

"Now, you still read my diary, so I say we're even," she

said, flicking her hair back and crossing her arms. Melanie scowled back.

"We had a reason to distrust you. You seemed to hate all of us," Melanie softened, "But... we were wrong. You are an amazing person, Ashley. You deserve friends. And friends deserve you."

For a fraction of a second, Ashley's angry features crumbled to sad defeat. Then, her face masked to cold stone and she glowered at the trio.

"I went into your tent to see if one of you had anything to help me get out of here and run far, far, away from all of you."

Melanie didn't feel angry anymore. She couldn't feel angry. She had two best friends, yes. But Ashley was someone totally different. Since birth, Ashley McMallan had been decided to be someone who could almost never have friends. Almost. And that "decision," her bond, was ruining her life. Melanie took a step closer to Ashley and put a soft hand on her shoulder.

"Ashley," she said, "You don't need to escape. And you won't ruin anyone's lives. You may think that your "bond" defines you, but it doesn't. It may be what everyone sees in me, or in Hazel. But you can make it so that people see what you really are. You shouldn't let your bond control you. Use it as a guide and then control your own life and make your own decisions. And I know that I sound cheesy," added Melanie, blushing, "But you can't be like this anymore."

Melanie clasped something in her hand. She handed Ashley a bracelet made of pure gold. Hazel gasped.

"Melanie! What are you—"

Cora shook her head.

"Melanie! No—"

Ashley blinked like she didn't believe what was happening.

"Melanie!" she said, her voice sounding just like someone in denial, "Merlin gave that to you. Not me. My bond has nothing to—"

"You shouldn't let your bond define you," Melanie said patiently, " If the world said you would be slow at making friends, then let it say that. But don't you realize, everyone wants to be your friend and you turn them down because of something that you think will lead your life. Your bond isn't supposed to control you or force you to change. Your bond can help you with choices but it shouldn't make the choices for you. And Ashley, I trust you. That's all that matters. Even if you spoke badly of me or snooped through my tent, The Woods Master would never think I entrusted this to you. Take the bracelet, Ashley."

Cora and Hazel's strangled expressions changed to

smiles. Ashley's eyes glowed... but then dimmed.

"No," she said, lowering her eyes to the ground. I was born cursed and I will curse your lives if I come into them. That's my destiny: stay out of people's business and let them be the heroes. I'd mess everything up if I tried to befriend them."

Melanie shook her head.

"No—"

But Ashley wasn't listening any more. Cora and Hazel looked at Ashley with pleading expressions. How did my speech not work? Thought Melanie. How did Ashley not understand? Melanie knew Ashley was still hiding something. She wanted to ask about how it was even possible that Oliver was her father. She wanted to ask her what she knew about her ancestry now. She wanted more answers. But now wasn't the time.

Something cried out outside of the tent. Cora reached for her sword and Hazel gripped her medical equipment. Melanie shoved the bracelet into Ashley's hand and sprinted into the night. The same scream echoed louder this time. Melanie's heart thudded as loud as the scream itself. It was coming from Natalie's tent.

"Natalie!" gasped Melanie, ripping open her mother's tent and stampeding in, heaving breaths. In the corner of the room, Natalie was curled into a ball, shoulders hunched and arms gripping her legs tightly.

"Natalie! Are you alright?"

Natalie whimpered a bit and looked behind Melanie's back. She followed her gaze and found herself face to face with a glob of hovering paint, resembling a sleek black bullet. Melanie froze. She had read it in the book on the birth of Riverhaven. The Woods Master's weapons. Melanie could hear Hazel, Cora, and Ashley's footsteps, and Melanie gurgled. Please, she begged, don't come in. They came in, arms raised and completely unaware of the paint bullet. Melanie held in a scream and pointed her shaking finger to it. The three girls halted and lowered their raised fists. The bullet circled each and every one of the girls, lurching forward —in which Ashley squealed in terror— and then calmly veering back, as if enjoying the paralyzed group.

"Don't... move," whispered Natalie, "I'm Riverhaven's caretaker. I know what to do."

Natalie straightened and slowly started walking, arm poised in her front like a blast of light would come out. Melanie was right, mostly. A blast of papery orange light exploded from Natalie's outstretched hand, an unbearable amount of pressure that launched Natalie backwards. Melanie ran to her and caught Natalie, stumbling backwards from the weight, and... the black paint bullet was gone.

"How did you do that?" asked Hazel, blinking repeatedly to make sure that what she was seeing was real. But Natalie was still limp in Melanie's arm, breathing heavily, her work ripping the consciousness out of her. A gash in the tent from where the bullet had come in was peeling to the side and the sound of slippery grass sounded outside of it.

"That's weird…" murmured Melanie. And weird it was. The sound grew louder, now sounding like scraping nails on a chalkboard. Melanie winced at the sound and closed as much of the tents peeling drapes as possible. But the noise just kept getting louder. The tent collapsed on the girls. Melanie heard Cora yell for Hazel. She saw Hazel nervously trying to set the tent back up while Ashley crawled on the floor, screaming like a little girl.

"The grass is getting my new dress wet!!"

The sound suddenly stopped. The tent slowly rose back to how it was, though with a couple grass stains and a huge dent in the side. Melanie gripped Natalie, trying to wake her up. Hazel ran up to Melanie, a bit dazed, clinging onto Cora's arm so forcefully that Cora was gritting her teeth in pain. Ashley stood in the corner, rubbing grass off of her dress and fussing with her frizzy braid.

"Did you hear that noise?" asked Cora, picking at the place that Hazel had just let go of.

"Yeah…" said Melanie, voice trailing off. She clutched

Natalie and sauntered to the back of the tent. "Guys! There are more bullets!"

Fifty paint globs came rushing through the tent, ripping right through it and cornering a girl. In the rush, Melanie had dropped Natalie who was laying in the middle of the tent, the only one who was unguarded by a paint bullet. Melanie had to get to her. But the 5 paint bullets that were cornering her were slowly morphing into a wall, turning solid and lurching forward to attack if you moved. The paint bullets around Ashley were razor sharp and closer to her than to anyone else. Tears were forming in Ashley's eyes and shc was looking at Melanie, silently saying: help me. But Melanie didn't know how to help. The paint hovering above Hazel charged at her and pricked her at all sides. Hazel yowled in pain, thrashed at the paint, stinging wounds forming on her skin. Cora's paint bullets wrapped her in a cocoon of paint, leaving her face untouched. Ashley, Melanie, and Natalie were the only ones that hadn't been harmed yet. Melanie gulped. She was the leader. She was supposed to know what to do. But no ideas came to mind and Melanie found herself hyperventilating. Melanie looked down and saw that Natalie's eyes were fluttering open. Natalie was slowly lifting herself from the ground, eyes peered at the now hundreds of paint bullets in her tent. She raised her hand, but Melanie stopped her:

"Natalie! However you do that, you can't. You don't have enough strength."

Natalie didn't even deny. She just nodded and looked out of the torn fragments of her tent. She gasped. That was when an navy-cloaked woman, with hazelnut hair and olive skin came walking in. Melanie narrowed her eyes. She looked a lot like Natalie, except her hair was in tiny braids. In fact, she looked exactly like Natalie.

"Sister," she said in a calm voice, "It's good to see you again."

Chapter 36
The Realm Jumper

Natalie's mouth felt dry. Her head was whirring, dizzy. She shook her head, swallowing the rise of emotions.

"Rea-Rea"

Natalie tried to say Realm Jumper but it came out more like croaks and breaths. Hazel and Cora both looked at each other.

"That's the lady who captured us and put us in the oak tree!" exclaimed Cora, her body swiveling around, trying to get the paint globs off of her. "You witch!"

The Realm Jumper smiled sadly.

"Hazel, Cora, I am the Realm Jumper."

Melanie grunted as loud as she could, trying to get The Realm Jumper's attention. For some particular reason, she felt highly offended that the lady was ignoring her, Ashley, and Natalie, her own sister. The RealmJumper pretended that she didn't notice.

"I'm... sorry... for y'know capturing you. It's just... I had to. I've been robbed of money and..."

"And so you go around capturing girls and making it look like it was all for a good cause?" spat Melanie. Natalie stirred and looked at Melanie threateningly, telling her to calm down. She could calm down later. Melanie had watched her dad as he explained his betrayal, she had read a letter which made her think that Natalie had betrayed her, she had seen the last sign of her two friends in her palm, she had nearly lost all of the things that she fought so hard for. And now this lady came and said that she was perfectly fine with this, that stealing someone was fine. Because in Melanie's head, all she was thinking about was how people kept taking away the things she loved, without even considering the effect on someone besides themselves and the thing that they took. She wasn't going to lose her only family again.

"Look," said The Realm Jumper, "I was once like you…"

Melanie glared down at the woman. Hazel and Cora were still struggling, but a little less vigorously. Why did she pull the I was once like you card; I was once naive too sentence. Natalie was still silent and Ashley was gaping at her in a mix of hurt, surprise, and uttermost confusion.

"You are the one who took care of me under the volcano in Hawaii," said Ashley, tight lipped. The Realm Jumper nodded.

"I was wealthy at the time. Plus, I had a reason to care for you. And it wasn't only because Oliver left you." The Realm

Jumper glanced down.

Ashley stuttered and tried to speak but the words seemed to be ripped out of her.

"I don't understand," said Melanie. That was when she noticed the dim look in Natalie's eyes. Natalie slowly lifted herself and walked up to the Realm Jumper. Her voice was crisp and commanding, a tone Melanie had never heard from Natalie:

"Release them," she said.

The black bullets of paint were still squirming and rippling in their positions.

"But... The Realm Jumper doesn't control those eels," began Melanie.

"The Wwoods Master does..." finished Ashley, her voice hushed. The group of captives finally noticed what The Realm Jumper kept looking at" her hands. They were trembling, each finger wiggling faster than Melanie could see. It all clicked in.

"You're afraid of the Woo—"

The Realm Jumper sprinted into the air and landed on Melanie's chest, collapsing her to the ground and placing a hand on her mouth, muffling the rest of her words. Natalie gurgled and Hazel and Cora rushed to help but The Realm Jumper took out a long orange staff, crackling with electricity. Everyone stood back from the lady in orange atop their quest leader. The Realm Jumper, instead of frying Melanie alive, hurriedly scraped at the grass and formed a sentence.

HE CAN HEAR. THE PAINT IS HIS WEAPON.

Everyone in the room dawned with understanding, but Melanie understood the real message that The Realm Jumper was saying. Exterminate the paint, and they could talk with no interruptions or ambushes from the man who sent the paint to begin with. She nodded at Cora. Cora, still stuck in her cocoon of paint, tried, and failed to pick up the rusty metal sword from the floor. The Realm Jumper approached and, with a sword called Excalibur, once belonged to Cora before being stolen, and pierced through some paint to hand it to her.

"Excalibur...!" Cora stopped mid sentence and pulled as much of the sleeves from her grey sweatshirt that were visible up. She shifted her weight so her silky black hair tucked behind her ear. It all looked pretty funny since, from Melanie's point of view, she was seeing her friend trying to walk and handle a sword while wrapped in a thick layer of murderous paint. Cora's elbows from inside her paint cocoon buckled and she spread them out with so much force that the paint exploded off of her... but not for long. They reformed around her wrists and formed into duct tape. Excalibur clanged to the ground just when everybody else's wrists magically became bound by paint duct tape. Everyone stood there, shocked and twisting at the tape. The harder Melanie wiggled around, the stronger and tighter the tape became. Then, out of nowhere, Natalie saved the day:

"To tear duct tape, you need to put lateral stress on the cross part of it..."

"And you do that by," chimed The Realm Jumper, voice trailing while a faraway look crossed her eyes. She never finished her sentence.

"Okay everybody," said Natalie calmly, the same expression on her face, "Raise your hands above your heads..." Everybody did, Ashley biting her lip nervously. "And now, in one single fast movement, swing your arms down and try to get past your rib cage." At once, everyone swung their hands down and slowly, small tears appeared on the duct tape. The tape around their arms eventually broke off and scattered into a bunch of razor sharp paint bullets, circling the tent. Cora grabbed the hilt of her sword and hoisted it above her head, Hazel grabbed the nearest object: a green tube made of plastic, Natalie gingerly swept to the to with her cloak in hand and a lasso of rope swung on her shoulder, The Realm Jumper joined the circle and took out a bunch of green circular discs from her identical coat to Natalie's, and Ashley finally walked over timidly and took out a couple hairpins and some hair ties from her hair. Melanie stepped in front of the circular like a leader protecting them and faced the bullets, weaponless, but clever and full of ideas. Cora charged at the paint bullets with a battle cry and slashed them into shreds, Hazel swung the tube at anything that came near her, spearing them like a kabob or simply hijacking them like an ax, Ashley screamed helplessly when the paint came at her and pointed at her heart. But then, just as it was about to hit her, she withdrew a hairpin out of her pocket and slingshot it with her hair tie at the bullet, smearing it onto the other side of the tent. She grinned.

"I can also be pretty smart…"

Melanie unsheathed her sword and deflected paint that was heading her way, jumping and kicking in marvelous speed. Natalie and The Realm Jumper stood together, back to back, never leaving each other's side. A huge mass of paint sloshed at The Realm Jumper and Natalie swished her navy cloak out majestically and swooped the deadly bullets out of the air, twirling the cloak around until all Melanie saw was a blur of navy. The Realm Jumper smiled at Natalie gratefully. The exchange warmed Melanie's heart. Natalie had been lonely. Her sister was back. But Melanie's moment of joy didn't last long. More and more black paint was coming in, sharper than any knife in the world. Melanie kicked at some, punched others, and when the moment came, she threw back her head and roared.

Melanie never considered herself as fierce or intimidating. She herself could be intimidated easily. But something inside her throughout these past days had flipped a switch inside of her. She had found her strengths, a family, and a super cool sword. Nothing could stop her now. Her voice echoed loudly in the woods and this time, her voice wasn't raspy at all. It was loud and defining.

The tent shredded to pieces and a raging monster came in. Everyone froze. It had green scaly arms that were shooting sparks of venom, a long black tail that whipped around its charcoal black face, teeth bared, pointy fangs sticking out of its army green lips. But that wasn't all. Millions of spiders scurried around its shredded grey rag of a dress, hissing loudly. Melanie noticed Ashley clutching her heart.

"I have... arachna... phobia!" Ashley spluttered, hyperventilating and clutching Melanie's arm so firmly that her knuckles were white. Melanie gulped. Having this thing in the room was bad enough, but if phobias were going around, things would get much worse. Luckily, the monstrous animal was on their side.

"Please creature," said Melanie, "Help us get rid of these deadly paint bullets."

The monter didn't move.

"What are you waiting for?!" croaked Melanie, hysteria rising as more and more paint bullets rushed in. Natalie and The Realm Jumper's eyes clicked and some secret understanding passed between them. Natalie approached the monster and gave her a warm smile, placing both of her hands on the creature's side and closed her eyes tightly, as if she was giving the creature a part of herself. Tendrils of fiery orange smoke curled off Natlie's fingertips and dissolved into the monster's skin. The Realm jumper pulled down the hood of her cloak and placed her arms on the monster's hair and did the same as Natalie, though the orange smoke coming from her was lighter and less powerful. The monster was paying attention now. It nodded at the two sisters and they three stood together in a dramatic pose. All of them closed their eyes harder than before and raised their arms up and down in a flowing motion until orange smoke had embraced them. They then thrusted their hands down and stuck their heads high into the air. The smoke spiraled them like the tip of a drill, spinning until Melanie's eyes stung. Slowly, the orange color doubled in size and intensity until Melanie couldn't see the trio anymore. The bullets still hovering above their captors, slowly started to stretch and slip into the tornado of orange fog. The black eels gave off squalls and horrible high pitched noises that rattled inside of Melanie's ears. The fog was now the size of the monster itself and any trace of a black paint bullet was gone, hidden beneath the layers of smoke. Then, just like nothing had happened, the smoke vanished, leaving a coughing monster and two sisters standing side by side.

***

"So..." said Melanie, sitting cross legged in the remaining debri of Natalie's tent, "Your name is Rhea?"

The Realm Jumper looked away from her gaze with Natalie and the secret understanding that was passing through their eyes and nodded.

"How exactly did you defeat the paint?" asked Ashley challengingly, "You just made smoke appear..."

Natalie smiled, completely unintimidated.

"Well, The Woods Master morphed the paint out of his own anger, hate and greed for power, right?" Everyone nodded except for The Realm Jumper, impatient, "Well, to defeat hate... you simply shower it in love."

Melanie thought about that for a while. A faint and faraway shout came from the distance. Melanie ignored it and kept thinking. There was one thing she still didn't understand.

"How exactly did you and the creature shower the paint in love?" she asked.

"Well, first. Rhea and I gave a small bit of our power into the creature, to make it stronger and also to say that we come in peace and will stand by her side during any danger she may face."

Ashley gagged and said:

"Stand by that thing?"

Everyone ignored her which clearly did not feed her ego.

Natalie continued. The yell from behind her was a bit louder this time.

"Rhea and I both thought of amazing memories of each other and anything closeby and helped the monster destroy the paint by turning that happiness into something that could swallow the bullets whole. But that isn't important. What is, is that Rhea had no choice to capture Hazel and Cora. Someone took away her money and I know who."

"You do?" gasped Rhea, Hazel, Cora, and Ashley. A wave of dread chilled Melanie to the bone.

"The Woods Master!" she exclaimed, eyes wide, "He robbed you so that you would have to come to him for the money. He's been doing it to others too!"

Melanie remembered her quick and mysterious conversation with the Serpent With No Tail. He had said: "I'll make sure to mention your location. It will sssserve usssse." At the time, Melanie hadn't understood him and let the sentence roll off of her. But she understood now. That was how he had known her location. He was paying people the money he had robbed from them to find her. The Woods Master was taking all the villains in the forest and using them for something they already had. Melanie growled. How could anyone get away with something like that? Everyone else had the same expressions, which just riled her up even more. Then, the most unexpected thing happened. Ashley put a hand on her shoulder, giving her a sympathetic smile.

"But that's going to come to an end. Right, Melanie?"

Maybe it was that Ashley had suddenly become a bit nicer, or maybe it was the realization that her possibly new friend was right, or maybe it was the way everyone looked at her like she belonged and wasn't a foolish girl like how everyone used to think, Melanie smiled as another wave of noises came from behind her.

"Right!" she exclaimed. She waited for Natalie to give instructions or someone to take the lead, but everyone was looking at her, waiting.

"It's time for our team leader to take the lead!" exclaimed Hazel at last. Melanie felt a surge of power and happiness. The faint noise came again.

"Alright, we need to split up. Whatever The Woods Master is planning will be stopped now! Realm— I mean:

Rhea, I need you to relocate The Woods Master's hideout and send something back telling us where. Make sure it's something reliable and that won't get intercepted. Hazel, Cora, I know you guys and Ashley will both refuse this request and I still don't really know what I'm requesting. But I need you two to go find Oliver and bring him to me. Do not let him escape." Hazel and Cora both turned two shades lighter and shaked their heads vigorously.

"No."

"You don't know what you're asking us."

"I will no—"

But no one was more forceful than Ashley. She gripped a metal pole that hadn't collapsed like the reality of the situation was so horrible that she felt dizzy.

"You... can not send them." she said, gasping and shaking her head and fidgeting with everything.

"Look," Melanie said, sounding a lot like her father, "I don't know the problem between you four and I'm not going to ask. But we need Oliver. If you two don't go to find him, then I will."

Melanie knew that she was lying. She couldn't go find Oliver. But she didn't wait for a response. Melanie turned to Natalie, chin raised stubbornly and a very leader-ish look on her face.

"Natalie, you need to evacuate Riverhaven. You will be the only person they'd listen to."

Natalie frowned.

"Why are we evacuate—"

"Please," Melaniei said, "We don't have much time." Melanie finally met eyes with Ashley and took a breath in.She didn't really know how Ashley would react to what she was going to say next. She wasn't really sure if she liked the idea she had come up with. Well, it was too late now.

"Ashley, you're coming with me."

Everyone looked around like someone else had said it. Ashley looked thoroughly confused.

"Me?" she said, half amused and a bit disgusted. "Sorry, can't..." But Rhea had already run off with Briarrides stomping a racket behind her, Natalie had already mounted Sapphire into the air and disappeared, and Hazel and Cora had already trailed into the forest, grumbling something about: the worst job ever."

"So... uh... what are we doing?" asked Ashley finally, wishing that she could have any partner but Melanie, even the smelly dragon.

"We're going to sneak into the cave over there and save whoever has been yelling."

Chapter 37
The Worst Jobs Ever

Natalie simply despised flying. She didn't have the courage to mention that all of the times that she ended up in the air unwillingly. However, now... she could. When Natalie became caretaker, a unicorn had thrown her into the air magically and blessed her with happiness and eternal life, all the usual stuff. But this had been done after some of the acts of The Woods Master and this unicorn's horn was twisted and didn't work so well. Which means, Natalie ended up plummeting to her death... until Rhea created a blanket of air that caught her. Siblings are lucky that way. Natalie had never gotten over that and wasn't planning to.

"Sapphire, could you slow down a bit?" she asked, voice straining to a whisper. Sapphire immediately slowed and trotted through the air calmly. Natalie reassured herself over and over again:

"You're in good hands, Natalie," she said, "Sapphire is perfectly capable of flying slowly without dropping me."

Though every time she spoke, her palms just got slippery with sweat. Natalie gripped Sapphire and looked down. Bad mistake. Rows and rows of huge trees and a couple of buildings appearing in the distance seemed like ants to her. Natalie gripped onto Sapphire until the unicorn had to let out an annoyed whimper. Natalie straitened and closed her eyes. Another bad idea. When she let her eyelids slowly close, she felt dizzy and unbalanced and kept thinking that she was going to fall off. This resulted in more gripping to Sapphire's fur and the opening of Natalie's eyes. She sighed in relief when she saw that the town had come into view.

"Please land Sapphire," she said, voice no longer strained. Sapphire gently thumped to the cobblestone streets and Natalie rushed into the townsquare screaming:

"Evacuate the town! Evacuate the town! We're all in danger!"

***

Rhea was a lot like a fugitive. She was on the run a lot, in a different way than what you might think. Her town, Riverhaven, had never paid much attention to her until she decided that she had wanted to live in the woods. A couple crazy people who didn't know who they were facing tried to come at her and rob all her possessions. She had quite a lot of money after all. Only one person ever succeeded: The Woods Master. And it was now time for her to help take him down.

Running through a forest filled with unsuspected

surprises was like stealing candy from a baby for Rhea. In no time, her orange cloak was slightly torn form all the tree branches she had crashed into without caring. Rhea tripped and gripped a branch to steady herself. Rustling from the bushes awoke her senses. She tore the branch out of the tree and raised it.

"Show yourself!"

Rustle.

"Show yourself!"

Another rustle.

Something behind her touched the tip of her back and Rhea swung the stick without thinking, whacking whatever touched her in the head and throwing him backwards. Rhea turned to see a snake with no tail groaning, slumped at the side of a tree.

"The tailless snake," murmured Rhea.

The Woods Master was at it again.

A flickering light appeared behind Rhea and she turned. Her highness The Animal Guardian appeared behind her.

"Your highness!" said Rhea.

"We don't have much time, dear. You know me and my duty to protect animals. A lot of lives are in danger. You need to find the—"

Something slashed through the projection and The Animal Guardian disappeared. A man covered in slick black paint approached Rhea. She froze. The Woods Master. Rhea stood taller and breached a war cry, spearing the long spiky stick into the air, crashing into The woods Master and making a gash in his bdy. Rhea, if you don't know, has also been known as The great Warrior, literally. No one had seen anyone better. And The Woods Mater was powerful which therefore surprised her how easily her job had been done. She was mistaken. The stick clattered to the ground and his wound got smoldered in paint, and he looked up, eyes gleaming evilly.

Oh no, thought Rhea. How can you kill someone who's unkillable?

Just find his hideout and then you can run, she thought. The Woods Master smiled as he had read her thoughts.

A bind of solid metal wrapped tightly around her wrists and legs. A coating of what looked like moving kinetic sand covered her mouth. Rhea gurgled, astonished. A small fire appeared behind her. Rhea screamed, only to hear it muffle through her gag. The Woods Master walked away, flicking his hands to make the fire get closer and closer. Rhea could feel the beat of her heart turn into a racecar. For a moment, Rhea forgot that she was a double creation and could manipulate fire. Luckily, she did just in time.

Rhea was about to perform a type of magic that could wipe people unconscious for days and even kill someone who has had no training. Rhea let herself fall rigid. The fire consumed her which should have killed her on the spot but just seemed to bathe her in smoke. Rhea was already using a lot of her power, transporting water from the magical underwater kingdom of terishatopia and dousing herself in it internally, making her immune to the fire. That should have ripped the consciousness out of her. But Rhea had spent years under the training of multiple leaders: The Animal Guardian, her mother, and even Natalie herself. Rhea bit her lip, blood trickling out of her now split lip. Rhea forced herself to bring out every drop of magical water in a 40 mile radius to soak into her skin. Her eyes drooped and her sweat turned ice cold. Her temples were throbbing and red spots were dancing around her vision. Rhea felt herself starting to get dizzy and cried out in the most stranded voice anyone had ever heard. She then did the impossible. Out of nothing, only using her imagination, she strung out muscles and bones from her body, which regenerated afterwards, and used those to make the fire hotter, and hotter and HOTTER until Rhea felt the metal in her arms slowly melt away. The fire disappeared in a flash and Rhea crumpled to the floor in a heap of exhaustion. Right before consciousness slipped away, she murmured:

"Worst ... J-job... eve—"

***

Hazel and Cora weren't in a good mood. They couldn't be, not when the're assignment was to find Oliver.

"Worst..."

"Job..."

"Ever..."

They continued walking. But where were they walking to? They still didn't know. The instructions that Melanie had given them weren't that clear: Go into the woods, find Oliver. The woods were endless, so vast and   , there wasn't even a starting point.

"Worst..."

"Job..."

"Ever..."

In reality, it was the worst job ever. Oliver and the two girls had a history, and it wasn't a good one. No, not at all. Hazel tried to keep the awkward silence at bay by ranting on about one thing or the other. Cora's eyes stayed fixed on the tree that it seemed like they kept passing. They both sighed in unison. When they found the boy, Melanie would have questions, and, like everything with an answer, she was going to know them soon.

"If I was Oliver," said Hazel, "Where would I be?"

"Anywhere where humans weren't" murmured Cora in an immediate response.

"Alright then," said Hazel, lips pressed in a way that said I really don't want to do this, "I know where he is."

She took out a small squared compass, lined with swirls of blue and purple and specks that represented stars. She pressed the red button that was below it. Merlin's bearded, withered face appears.

"Merlin!" Cora said, eyes brimming with relief and happiness, "You're okay!" The last time the girls had seen him, he had been rushed to the ER.

"It is good to see you two girls," said Merlin, his warm deep voice sounding scratchier than usual, "Why have you called me?"

Hazel took a deep breath and spread out her swirly green skirt.

"I don't want to pass as rude Merlin, especially in your condition, but I know what you've done for Oliver. Please tell us where you've hid him."

Merlin cleared his throat.

"You two are clever. But I've sworn under the double creation oath. I can not tell you."

Cora stepped up, her sweet expression hardening.

"This isn't about an oath. This is a matter of national security. If we don't know where he is, then Riverhaven is in danger. And Merlin, I know that you have always ended up being wiser than everyone, and even if the most powerful oath is involved. Please Merlin. You know my relationship with Oliver. It is so serious that I have to go this far to find him."

"Are you questioning the double creation oath? Are you saying that all double creations and the magic holding our world together isn't as important?"

Cora gulped. If she said yes, then her life may as well be over. She looked at Hazel, both of them mirroring terrified expressions.

"I-I"

"Yes!" said Hazel. "I'm questioning the oath."

Cora spun around to her friend, eyes blurred by the shocked tears pouring out of them. She shook her head.

"No-no!"

Merlin was frozen on the other side of the projection. Hazel's own eyes flooded with salty tears and she hugged her friend. A slimy twisting rope wrapped around her and pulled her down. Cora screamed. Hazel let the bridge between her tears collapse and they streamed down her soft cheeks.

"YOU DARE QUESTION THE OATH?" roared a horrible scratching voice.

Merlin unfroze from his petrified daze.

"HAZEL!"

Merlin thrust his hand backwards, let out a noise so strong and powerful, it seemed impossible it could come out of a mouth like his.

Cora's vision was obscured by the deepest blue in the universe, overcoming any type, even the darkest pits of the ocean. She heard a roar and a sound like a rope snapping. And then she saw Hazel freed, crying and laughing. Cora rushed to her friend.

"Merlin?" asked Hazel suddenly.

They both turned to see the projection from where Merlin had sat flicker and the man who had saved them, sprawled onto the floor, scraggly breaths just managing to escape from his mouth.

Chapter 38
Oliver

Hiding from people is like cutting onions. You know that you'll cry when you cut them but you do it anyway. That was the quote of my life.

As I contemplated that, visions of horror clouded my brain. Die... leave... encased... explodes. Words that wouldn't leave my head. I was jolted back to the present, screaming. My dark eyes gleamed dangerously like every single time this would happen. The image of The Woods Master grabbing Ashley by the neck was tattooed into my brain, the voice of the evil man still echoing:

"Oliver, I have finally wrapped the town in my paint bullets. Everyone there is encased. There will be no survivors. And definitely no witnesses here."

I blinked and my journey to the future ended. I felt like he was going insane. I hadn't even felt emotional, yet I was still brought back. This shouldn't be happening, I thought. Something is really wrong here, with everything. I slammed the ringing in my ears, screaming as I tried to erase everything I had seen but was not meant to. My head was pounding so loudly that I hadn't heard the footsteps arriving at the cave. A young girl ran into the cave and stopped at the sight of me, aghast. My eyes flashed and my entire body rang with panic. I shuddered as visions of explosions, dead mythical animals, and dirt covered humans filled up my brain, that one girl standing in the middle of it.

"It's you," I gasped.

The girl tried as best as she could to pick me up but I pushed her away screaming as more visions flooded into my head: the girl bowing down to an animal goddess, the girl running into the forest in distress as she carried his best friend's limp body, the same girl struggling to escape from the woods master as his paint encased her.

"LEAVE NOW."

I fell down, pounding the floor.

"I need to get you out of here," she exclaimed, "You're injured."

The large gash in my arm felt numb and painless as visions of the girl stampeded through my head.

"You're the girl from the future. I've seen you before. You're in danger!"

The young girl looked panicked as she listened to my words, confused.

"Please, you need to cooperate. I'm trying to help you."

No, he thought. No, no, no. She had made a personal connection with me. Which meant...

My eyes slashed into the darkness and I fell unconscious as another vision of the future crowded my brain.

The young girl let me go, staring.

"Wait a minute, I know someone whose eyes do that," she gasped.

My brain was overridden with a vision of this girl in Merlin's cabin, rummaging through his bedroom, in a desperate need for something. The roof had crashed on top of her and she fell to the floor, nearly unconscious as a giant snake with no tail came in, grabbed her by the leg and disappeared. Someone in his vision was screaming for the girl but it was muffled.

I snapped back into the present again, screeching louder and louder as the vision drove me to the brink of insanity.

"Oh my god!" The girl gasped, "You-you just fell unconscious, like into a slumber. And I know you— You're from the..."

Right at that moment another girl came running in, her orange hair mopped with sweat.

"Melanie, what's wrong?! I heard.

My heart stopped right there and then.

***

Melanie was so utterly confused. This boy that seemed to be going insane was the same one that was at Merlin's at some point. His eyes had flashed dangerously just like they did moments ago. Melanie had thought it was just the eerie light but the second his eyes flashed, he seemed to go into some sort of nightmare. This boy was Oliver. Yet Oliver seemed to have gone insane, talking about Melanie being in his visions or from the future or something. And if that wasn't confusing enough, Ashley walked in. And after reading her diary entries, Melanie knew this was bad.

"WHAT?!" Ashley bellowed.

Oliver was deadly silent for the first time since Melanie walked in, his head on the ground and his eyes dull and seemingly lifeless.

"What in Merlin's beard is going on here?!

Ashley stormed her way up to Oliver, shouting in his face.

"Get UP. Get up NOW, you fool!"

Melanie wasn't even sure if Oliver could hear her. He was unconscious again, twitching and mumbling words like:

"Destroyed...won't work..."

"Too late... Melanie...Sacrifice...Danger ... Ashley escape... HEART..."

"HEART...HEART!"

Ashley wasn't paying attention to that, screaming her head off at a boy who wasn't listening. But Melanie was in a state of distress. Oliver seemed to have lost his sanity. And if Merlin was right when he said that Oliver is the key to taking down the Woods Master then he needed professional help soon. Because even if Oliver was hiding for some reason, he would understand the safety of Riverhaven and Ashley relies on him (somehow).

"Ashley, you have gotta calm down... ASHLEY, can't you see that Oliver is unconscious again?"

Ashley looked at Melanie, tears staining her cheeks and swallowed . Melanie grabbed Oliver by the arms, sprinkled some fairy dust around him (that Merlin had secretly stuffed in her backpack ages ago), which made Oliver float in mid air, weightless. Melanie pushed him through the air and out the cave. Ashley was walking mindlessly behind Melanie, her stone cold eyes so intensely interested in the floor she could have written a love song about it.

"What do we do with him?" Melanie asked.

Ashley shook her head.

"I really don't know. I don't really know anything about him anymore. I don't understand any of his choices."

"You must know one person who knows him well enough to snap him out of insanity," Melanie insisted.

"We could go to Merlin's," Ashley replied bitterly, "he and Oliver are best friends..."

Oliver and Merlin are close friends? I mean, it makes sense in the way that Merlin praises Oliver when he so far sounds like a crazy person. But Melanie was then again still confused as to why Oliver was fourteen years old but somehow Ashley's father. But Melanie actually realized how perfect it would be to ask Ashley about it since she clearly needed it off her chest and the answer might help Melanie understand why Oliver was acting the way he was.

"Why is Oliver your father? I mean, I'd ask how but in the woods anything is possible. How can he be fourteen and you be thirteen? That's not really possible..."

Ashley looked up. "I-I don't actually know. You gotta believe me... One day he was a regular forty five year old man and then the next night he was sick and kept passing out and going to bed, and when I fell asleep, something—I don't know what— happened and I woke up and there he was, fourteen and shuddering, screaming, and gasping for breaths like he had gone insane."

Woah, that seemed helpful but also incredibly problematic at the same time.

"Are you literally saying that he passed out and was suddenly this fourteen year old boy who had gone insane?"

"Not really," said Ashley, "I mean he was constantly sick. Oliver is a huge introvert, never talks to anyone. Just like me. But he passes out anytime he seems to be around other people or if he's around anyone at all. It started with him randomly falling asleep, which is normal in the woods because it reflects a big aura and some people who are developing their bonds can get overwhelmed by it. But then he'd lock himself in his room. And then he started to wake up panicking and out of breath. I had to constantly calm him down.

"Oh my gosh"

That's all Melanie could say. Oliver was also passed out when she saw him, just like how Ashley described: slowly going insane. And the only real person who could fix this is—

Melanie took out the blue and purple compass, which would lead her directly to Merlin.

"Ok, well let's fix this."

Ashley looked down at the grass again.

"I really don't know if we ca—"

"Oh my god Ashley. We're here... in the Trenside

Thicket. A literal walking fairytale. I've seen a troll the size of four tomato cans capture me. I've seen melted wax save my unicorn's life. We can find some potion to help Oliver."

"Ok, yeah! You're right. We can get there."

Suddenly, Ashley grabbed Melanie's arm who was holding Oliver and started running probably faster than the speed of light.

"GAAAAAAAAAAAAAAAAAAAAAAAAAAAAAAAAAAAAAAAAAAAAAAAAAAAAAAH" screamed Melanie.

"WWWWWWHATTT IS HAAAAAPPENING," yelled Ashley.

They were speeding their way through trees. Melanie felt so dizzy as the trees turned into green blurriness around her. When Ashley finally stopped, they were in front of Merlin's apartment. Melanie sat down and hurled into a bucket which had magically appeared in her bag.

"What in the world just happened?" gasped Ashley.

"I don't know."

They looked at each other nervously and walked up to Merlin's door, Oliver floating behind them. Melanie noticed how the door was open and tentatively tiptoed inside. On the couch sat Natalie, her thin eyebrows scrunched up nervously.

"So? Did you evacuate the town?" asked Melanie.

"Everyone has been put on dragons and will be flown

into New York. I came back to check on Merlin. He had an encounter... with the Double Creations Oath."

"Oh. My. WHAT?" gasped Ashley.

"Um... what's that?"

"It's the darkest pit of magic that there is. You know what a double creation is. Well The Double Creation was the first one in the world and the founder of Riverhaven. And The Double Creation is practically a spirit and so insanely powerful that if you swear on the "Double Creation Oath" and break that promise you made or if you challenge the Oath as to say that what you are speaking of is higher than the darkest and greatest magic in the universe, you will literally be sucked off this earth and never to be seen again. Ever."

"That's... insane. But... What does Merlin have to do with it?" asked Melanie.

"Well," said Natalie, "Hazel challenged it."

"No," gasped Melanie.

"Yeah. And Merlin volunteered to be taken instead, which has never happened in the history of The Trenside Thicket. That will definitely make it into a story from the Woods Pen."

"Are you saying Merlin's gone?"

"No. I have no idea what, but Merlin must have channeled his entire life source into this sacrifice because

Merlin and Hazel's power might have just been slightly big enough to make the Double Creation think that they don't need to be taken from this earth. Or... the Double Creation saw a reason they should live."

Melanie's heart glistened with hope. Maybe The Double Creation knew they were going to take down The Woods Master.

"But Merlin might need a couple years' rest."

"Years?"

"He definitely won't be able to fight in a year. He'll need to rest a lot, probably will need to use a cane for a while. But he is here, and can still provide you information about that weird guy who is floating behind you. And I assume this is why you're here."

Melanie giggled.

She walked with Ashley, Natalie, and the floating Oliver into Merlin's living room. Hazel and Cora were sitting on the couch, looking solemnly at Merlin. His skin looked five shades paler, the blue veins now as visible as fishes in clear water, and his hands shaking quietly. His eyes opened and he smiled a weak warm Merlin smile. Weakly, Melanie smiled back. Merlin noticed Oliver floating in the air and gave Ashley an amused look.

"Set him down," he said gently.

Slowly, Oliver's floating body fell to the floor. Melanie wasn't sure if it was her powers or Ashley's that lowered him.

"Merlin, I'm so sorry your sick," said Melanie.

"But you are explaining everything right now," interrupted Ashley.

"Ok."

"Can you please start with what happened when he turned fourteen randomly."

"That's a good place to start. And Melanie, you won't find this a surprise; all of this has to do with his Bond. Oliver gets visions. His Bond is that he can sometimes see into the future. It started with small little visions, he'd fall asleep for only about a minute and wake up. But slowly his trips to the future were longer and he'd constantly pass out around people. But the worst part wasn't the frequency or that he couldn't control it, it's what Oliver saw. Oliver didn't see visions of the future that were harmless, he started to see things that would happen years from when he saw them, or he'd see things so dangerous and traumatizing he could barely talk about it. If Oliver was around people, or too involved in something, or in danger, he'd randomly pass out and go into the future. It got so bad that at one point, the night he was with Ashley, he fell asleep. And while sleeping he traveled into the future for the longest time he had ever been in the future, and saw a vision that he said was going to happen to this young girl, who I believe is you Melanie. Whatever he saw was so scary that his bond glitched and he woke up as a fourteen year old. Because he had gone into the future so many times and seen so many things, his body simply malfunctioned and he got stuck in the past. He's still Oliver, but stuck in the body of a fourteen year old. The only problem was, his visions turned him into a sort of lunatic. He'd get out of a vision and be mumbling about it for days. Sometimes just words, but other times phrases. At one point he was on his bed, his whole body twitching and he told me: 'the giant...the giant arrives...end...it ends.' That was one of the reasons he distanced himself from everyone. When he turned into the body of a fourteen years old, he realized two things:

He could go insane and Ashley, you wouldn't know what to do. He didn't want you in that environment.

It seemed that Oliver would go into more visions when he was around people, but more importantly, if he was in danger or around people that would make him feel strong emotions. So technically, he's like..."

Merlin glanced at Ashley.

"He's like some people who let their Bond control them," said Melanie, with realization.

"Precisely," said Merlin, "He came to me asking if I could make a secret magical hideaway so he wouldn't be around people and maybe get less visions."

Ashley's eyes were glazed over. She looked like she wanted to speak, but no words formulated from her tongue. Melanie understood that feeling.

"Is there a way to make him control those visions?"

"That's something Oliver would have to figure out. No one ever really knows. But for now, Melanie, you have Oliver. You have got to get him to help you."

"Help me how?"

"He has had visions of you," mumbled Ashley quietly. Everyone turned to look at her. "Probably, I guess."

"He might know something about how to defeat the Woods Master and what you can do with your dad," said Merlin.

Melanie felt so dumb that she hadn't thought of this before.

"Of course! If he's had a vision of us destroying the Woods Master, maybe we finally do have the key to get rid of The Woods Master once and for all."

Melanie decided to wait a bit until it was around dinner time to wake up Oliver. Ashley had the idea to wake him up by brutally splashing ice cold water in his face and then banging something so that he'd definitely be alert. And, sadly, since Melanie had no other idea what else they could do, she opened up the tap and switched to the coldest setting. She put in some ice cubes and took out a pan. She turned away as she splashed the water on Oliver's face, feeling guilty; then she banged the pan.

"Gaghh?!! What the?"

Oliver rose from the couch sputtering and covering his ears.

"What just—"

Merlin, who was on an armchair next to the couch, said:

"Oliver, sit down."

"Oh, Merlin! It's you. I thought there was—"

Oliver noticed Ashley in the corner of the room.

"Merlin! I need to leave."

"It's too late," said Merlin wistfully, "I already told them everything."

"Oh..." he sighed, like he knew he couldn't really get mad about it.

"You can talk to Ashley about this later," said Merlin, "but for now I'd like you to reacquaint yourself with Melanie. She found you in the cave and got you out of your moment of insanity."

Oliver winced like those words were a dagger to the heart.

"It's nice to meet you!" said Melanie carefully.

"Yeah, whatever," he replied.

That was harsh.

"So, Oliver," said Melanie tentatively, "I've heard that you have been having a lot of visions about me."

Oliver said nothing. Melanie continued.

"Well, I'm not sure if you know about the situation out here but I'm trying to take down The Woods Master and—"

"Yes, I know," said Oliver, cutting her off.

"Oh, well... I was wondering you see, if we take him down, the Woods will be peaceful (or more peaceful then it is right now) and then you'll have the room and the time to figure out how to control your outbursts and be with Ashley again! But for that we need you to—"

"Tell you about my visions to see if they help you take down the Woods Master," cut in Oliver once again.

"Yeah... precisely!" said Melanie.

"But what's in it for me?"

"... excuse me?"

"You defeat your little nemesis, Riverhaven is safe, but what do I get?"

"I- I what?!"

"Oliver," said Merlin calmly, "This is different. Think about the bigger picture: everyone is safe to do what they've wanted. There is a guarantee that no one is going to cause trouble!"

"And? That's not my problem."

Melanie was simply flabbergasted.

"Dad!?" exclaimed Ashley, aghast.

"Ashley! I don't care about this Woods Master. He hasn't done anything to me! What is Melanie gonna do after she gets my information? Take it, get what she wants, become a hero and leave everyone to go back in the shadows?! Your problem isn't my problem!"

As Oliver was ranting on, shocking Natalie, Ashley, Melanie, and even Merlin, he abruptly fell to the floor, his eyes rolled back into his head as he dived into a vision.

Everyone gaped at him, scared out of their lives. Merlin was the only one who knew how to handle this.

"Melanie, bring a notepad, write down everything Oliver says. And I mean everything. Cora, get a bucket of cold water so we can wake him up after this. Natalie and Hazel, pay attention to what he is saying. This might be one of our last prophecies."

Slowly, strings of phrases started escaping Oliver's

mouth and Melanie got ready to jot them down.

"Melanie... He's coming. The Woods Master is coming... Pack up. Leave... find the woods ... Find the woods... things in Merlin's room ... MUST LEAVE."

Melanie dropped her pen and paper.

"You heard Oliver guys! I need to get stuff from Merlin's room and go into the Woods. That's where the Woods Master is."

Everyone was still trying to keep up with what was happening with Oliver. Melanie rushed out of the room and sprinted into Merlin's. She saw a backpack on the floor and grabbed it. On Merlin's night stand she saw a dagger. Reaching for it, Melanie looked and saw Ashley in the hallway running towards her screaming something urgently. But Melanie didn't have time to hear it. Melanie stuffed the dagger in her pocket, as Ashley kept running through the hall to get to her, screaming the same phrase louder and louder. That's when the roof split in half above Melanie, collapsing above her, forcing her to the ground. Protecting her head, Melanie screamed as more parts of the roof just fell onto her and the purple painted wood imploded. Then all the glass windows shattered and a single shard pierced her knee. Melanie looked up from the debris. The tailles snake, one of the Woods Masters' many minions stood in front of her.

"AAAAAAAAAAAAAAAH!"

Melanie wailed as she tried to get away, but the fallen roof had locked her to the ground. With a swoosh, he picked Melanie up as she scrambled to get out of his slimy embrace, and rocketed into the sky. Ashley finally ran into the room screaming as Melanie was lifted away.

Oliver gasped as he woke from his vision.

"NO! WAIT! THAT'S NOT A PROPHECY. IT'S A TRAP.

Chapter 39
Trapped

It had been a trap. It always was. And Melanie was dumb enough again to fall right into it. Literally. This was Oliver's vision. He saw Melanie being taken away, while Ashley tried to warn her. And her ignorance succeeded in making her fail once again. As the tailless snake rocketed into the air, Melanie had lost enough blood to make her stop squirming. And then he had all of a sudden dropped her in the middle of the Woods and disappeared. That's when the explosions started.

Melanie had sat down for a moment, trying to bear her surroundings and figure out where in the Thicket she was. But, surprise, surprise; it was just trees. So she went to inspect her wound which had opened more freely while trying to get away from the snake. And hot, sticky blood was spread over her leg. Her backpack was flung onto the floor a couple feet away from her, but she didn't have time to reach it. Because as she tried to stand up, a huge, circular ball of something-ness fell from the sky, obliviating the tree in front of her. With a giant CRASH! It exploded into flames, as dirt and what looked like—could it be gunpowder?—exploded from all sides. Melanie let out a shriek of fear and scrambled on the floor away from the tree. She heard another boom behind her and was nearly hit by a massive tree that had fallen just a foot from her body. She jumped up and sprinted, screaming as she tried to unleash energies to summon animals. A giant cannonball fell right next to her, grazing her foot and then exploded. Melanie ricocheted off the ground and slammed onto the floor. She felt her head violently jolt as she tumbled down. Everything around her was blurry and seemed to be shaking. Melanie felt dizzy and suddenly couldn't remember where she was or what was going on. Her eyelids fluttered to a close, and her head pulsed with jerks of pain. She felt like her arm was having a spasm, her lip seemed to be cut open, she was unaware of her surroundings; only hearing what she thought was a bomb. She groaned weekly as the noise shattered her earbuds. She knew she had a concussion. If only she could remember what the name of her kidnapper was again. Or what her own name was. Another loud explosion reverberated around her and Melanie blacked out.

***

Ashley sprinted back to the room where everyone was still waiting.

"Melanie—she—was—snake."

"We know," said Natalie, frantically pacing up and down the room.

Hazel and Cora were in a frenzy: clenching their fists and breathing intensely as their forehead creased with worry.

"Well," said Ashley, "We need to find her!"

"Are. You. Dumb?" wailed Cora, gripping Excalibur like she was ready to slice anyone's head off, "WE DON'T KNOW WHERE SHE HAS BEEN TAKEN. MIGHT'VE BEEN A HOUSE, A TOWN, A DIFFERENT COUNTRY! WE'D BE LUCKY ENOUGH IF SHE'S IN THE TRENSIDE THICKET. BUT WE ALL KNOW THAT'S AN ENDLESS VOID OF TREES,"

"Where are we going to even find her?"

"Let's all calm down." This was the first time that Merlin had spoken. "First, no matter where they are taking her, they could not have gotten that far anyways. And second, even though I bet this is the doing of the Woods Master, we are probably dealing with the tailless snake right now. He's so lazy that he doesn't have the energy to even slither around. He would not accept this job for the woods Master if he had to go far. Let's just take Briarrides and fly over the Thicket until we find her."

As Merlin said it, a giant, red dragon with silver wings swooped down outside of the apartment and thumped on the floor lightly. But being a huge dragon and all, it rocked the apartment a bit.

"Come on," said Natalie.

"You're coming too," said Ashley, pointing at Oliver who seemed to be in a state of confusion.

Hazel grabbed his arm and they all rushed down the steps, outside.

One by one, everyone got onto Briarrides back as Natalie was shouting directions at it. Merlin, still being very injured and needing to rest, was still coming down the stairs and told everyone he'd come but take a safer way. Oliver was babbling on, annoyed about not wanting to be here and how it was none of his business. But no one was paying attention to him as Briarrides soared up into the air.

Hazel and Cora were at the front, as far away from Oliver as they could be. They were giving him the evil eye the entire time as he complained about being here.

"Anytime I get involved, things don't end well. This isn't going to end well."

Natalie was scanning the ground from up high, looking for any sign of Melanie.

"I don't need to be here," mumbled Oliver.

"Would you please be quiet?!" shouted Cora, annoyed.

"Yes! You're being annoying," added Hazel.

"NO I AM NOT! FREEDOM OF SPEECH!" shouted Oliver back.

"I swear, Oliver I might just whip out my sword right now and—"

"Guys!" Ashley cut in.

As the four were arguing, Natalie saw smoke in the distance. Faintly, she heard a loud BOOM sound. Fearfully, she directed Briarrides to get closer. Oliver and the three girls were still fighting with each other as Natalie noticed multiple fallen trees.

"Guys..." she drawled nervously.

"You be quiet!"

"No you be quiet!"

"Ugh!"

"You ugh!"

"Guys ... Am I the only one who hears explosions?" Natalie said more frantically, seeing fires starting to blaze around what looked like—

"I have a very sharp sword, you know."

"I want to see you try to attack me. I'm 45, remember."

"Old man..."

"GUYS!"

Everyone stopped to look at Natalie.

"Am I the only one who sees fires surrounding fallen trees and a girl who looks unconscious on the floor?!"

Everyone but Oliver gasped in panic.

"Briarrides, get down to the floor. Now!!"

Briarrides landed and Natalie, Hazel, Cora, and Ashley jumped off, rushing to Melanie's unconscious body on the floor. She had three very scary looking purple bruises on her face. Her entire leg was covered in blood and her arm had shards of glass sticking on it. Burn marks blistered her fingers and her whole face was scarred like she had been in battle. Natalie let out a dry sob. Merlin, like usual, magically appeared behind them, making Natalie jump.

"Here."

He knelt down, slowly and with his cane, and dripped a golden liquid into Melanie's parched lips.

Her eyes, tentatively fluttered open and she groaned in confusion.

A fuzzy vision of a man in blue robes hovered straight in Melanie's face. She could feel a glaring light hitting her eyes and she winced. Yes, she definitely has a concussion.

"Stackaberry soup has healing properties. She'll be conscious but dazed, bewildered and in no shape to fight."

Stackaberry soup? Where had she heard that from? Melanie remembered the gold liquid and a sweet taste like pure sugar. She strained her neck enough to look at everyone.

"Melanie, can you hear me? What's going on?"

Melanie tried to answer, confused. This was Natalie, she thinks. Her ... mother; right! Next to her was ... She couldn't remember. All she could see was orange hair. Then she caught a little blurred flash of two very worried girls hovering above her in a state of panic. All she could think of was that they were her best friends.

"I'm Melanie," she stuttered. Even speaking hurt, "And I- I was dropped. There were explosions. It—"

"What is it?" questioned Natalie.

"I'm guessing," said Oliver, his arms crossed, "That it's like I said. It's all a trap. The Woods Master managed to create a fake vision for me where I made it seem like Melanie needed to go to Merlin's room. They captured her knowing we'd come too. And now that Melanie is almost dead—"

"Don't say that!"

"Now that she is almost dead and can't do anything, The Woods Master can now destroy Riverhaven using Melanie's father. And we will be there to get the first hit. He can't waste an opportunity to shove this in our faces so that the people who caused all these problems will now get to see him rise to power. I knew I shouldn't have gotten involved."

Everyone knew Oliver was right.

And just like that, in the snap of a finger, three hooded creatures emerged from Melanie's bleary vision. Hazel slowly lifted Melanie up so she could see, even though every bone in her body was aching in the worst possible pain. Her memory seemed to rush back to her as she saw them.

First came a man with shaggy ringlets of hair. His beard was so long and messy, he looked like an overgrown bush. His clothes were tattered rags and there was more mud on him than actual clothes. His look was completed with a nest of twigs and leaves laid on his head crookedly. His most memorable feature was the rotten stench of dead fish that encircled everyone, the toxic fumes flying free in the wind. He was the one and only: King Henry of The Monerines. Behind him, with his large net and short, prideful walk came a four foot tall goblin holding a giant dagger that didn't look like it would fit in his hands. He was the goblin who framed Melanie on live TV and almost killed and sold millions of rare creatures. Lastly, slithering behind them was the tailless snake, his smug, slimy expression staring right at Melanie. She staggered back. Her first three enemies were teamed up now to hurt her... or maybe they had been a team all along in the first place.

"We told you that we were going to get revenge, Melanie."

"After everything you've done to us."

"Destroyed our homes. Released our collections. Ruined our careers. Just simply annoyed us."

Melanie vaguely remembered running from all these bad guys, all of them promising revenge, seeking it. She shuddered.

"Wow, when you put it like that," said Cora confidently, "You make her sound like the bad guy."

Unsheathing her sword she ran towards the first one she saw: The Tailless snake and roared a battle cry. She sliced through the air, almost hitting him. But he dodged it fast.

"What are you waiting for!" she shouted behind her at the rest. "Get a bad guy and destroy him!"

Hazel grabbed a broken tree limb and rushed to help out Cora, swinging the limb with no self control, aiming to hit the snake straight in the stomach.

Natalie put on her cape, smiling in a brave but sinister kind of way and formed a ball of energy in her hand and shot it at King Henry. It pushed his crown off his head and he boiled with anger. He flicked his hand and five Monerines jumped up to attack Natalie. An orb of light propelled into two of them and hit the ground, unmoving. Hazel bonked the tailless snake on the head and Cora got her sword out but it was deflected by his tail. Melanie staggered in the middle of the scene. No one was attacking her but she knew she couldn't fight. She needed the energy to get to the sidelines but every single muscle in her body was shouting, her eyes were searching for their vision, her eardrums thumped loudly as more war cries sounded, and her skin was blistered and seared from fire marks. She tripped over herself and landed back on the floor, next to a tree. She stayed there, twitching as she tried to get her eyes to see straight. Everyone was still battling and it seemed to be that Melanie's friends were winning. Merlin was nowhere to be seen. Slowly, Melanie layed her elbow on the floor, and pushed herself up enough to deliriously get a look of what was behind her. There was a piece of rope wrapped around the tree she was laying against and two arms were tied together. Melanie gasped and then coughed as more ash got into her mouth. She realized that she still hadn't heard from Rhea since she had gone to … What had she gone to do? Melanie couldn't remember but did know that she was supposed to get some sort of signal. She rolled over and numbly untied the rope until it draped off the body it was attached to.

It was Rhea. In her hand was a rolled up piece of paper. Melanie picked it up and slowly unfolded it. Her vision was so obscured by weird flashes of light and oceans of blur that she couldn't understand it. That's when a giant hand snatched the paper from her hands. Melanie whirled around in confusion to see the Woods Master towering above her.

She went into full alarm mode, her brain flashing sirens of panic, not only because the Woods Master had finally arrived at everyone's weakest state, but because he was literally a giant. His legs were the size of miniature buildings. His head was like the biggest bowling ball in the world. He towered over Melanie and everyone who had been fighting before stopped, gaping.

"Oh, what is this that you're holding? A little note, huh? Well... let's read it."

All of Melanie's friends wavered in shock and stopped their fighting as The Woods Master ascended upon them.

"You're—you're giant!"

Melanie faltered when she tried to get up. Her whole throat was instantly parched and it was clogging up so fast she couldn't swallow. She was heaving breaths, trying to calm her rising hysteria but also not to let her cold, clammy hands and body temperature cause her to pass out again. Her mind was as blank as paper. The Woods Master opened up the letter with his now titanic fingers, smiling that evil sly grin that shook Melanie to her core.

"Run," it says. "The Tailless snake found me. I might not be conscious for some days unless I'm revived. But you need to get out here now, Melanie and crew. He's... Well, look at that," said The Woods Master, "She didn't have enough time to finish the letter before she passed out. Well done."

He nodded towards the Tailless snake.

"Oh," he flustered happily embarrassed. "It's nothing, really. I—"

"Ok that's enough, tailless snake. We don't want to hear more from you."

Chapter 40
The Battle

"Melanie. Don't you see? I have all the power now. Riverhaven banned me from entering but now I control all parts of it. Natalie, the person who is supposed to be protecting it is out and about, you guys can't stop me anymore, and you've left this place in disaster," said the Woods Master.

Melanie didn't know what to do. No matter how big of an army she had she couldn't defeat a giant.

"Plus," said the Woods Master, grinning. "I have some... assistance."

A normal sized figure emerged from the shadow of the giant Woods Master.

"Dad?"

"Walter!" gasped Natalie.

He looked different. His eyes were dark and dull, contrasting to his chalk-like pale skin. He looked so exhausted yet somehow still as composed as always.

"What did you do to him?" Melanie whimpered, aghast.

"What? Nothing. Walter?" The Woods Master beckoned him to come forward.

Melanie tried to scooch herself closer but the energy inside of her had dissipated at the sight of her father.

"Melanie," Walter said coldly.

Melanie knew this wasn't going to be an apology and he wasn't here for the reason she wanted him to be.

"This is what I need to do. I am doing this out of my free will—"

"No! No, you're not... Can't you see that he's using you? The Woods Master knows that you think you can only live with revenge. So he's using you to carry out his plan!" Melanie cried. "We all know you better than this. You do! You need to..."

Melanie bent over her shoulder and cried. She could feel Hazel's hand on her shoulder and Cora's fingers in hers. But everything else felt numb.

"Melanie," Walter's teeth were clenched tight, "I am not explaining this to you again. My motive is revenge. That is how I work. I wouldn't be alive without it and vengeance is my destiny in life. You yourself should know there is no way to fight destiny; or a Bond."

"Yes," the Woods Master prodded, "Ashley tried to

fight it but she'll still end up alone. Natalie," his expression went cold, "tried to ignore it. And yet here she is, about to die because of her daughter who carried on the power."

Cora took out her sword. Hazel grabbed a random nunchuck from the floor.

"And Oliver," The Woods Master smirked knowingly, "You tried the most. You tried everything you could to stay out of people's way. You did it because you didn't want to hurt anyone. But you hurt millions." Oliver looked away and Melanie felt a rush of anger.

"You don't know Oliver at all!" she screamed.

"Melanie..." he said, his tone serious.

"Oh really!" The Woods Master chuckled.

"Melanie, don't," Oliver warned.

"Oliver has been hiding many things from you Melanie. He knows the future and has seen a lot of people's past."

"And?!" Melanie choked out, her breathing getting faster until it felt like she had run a marathon. "Who does that hurt?"

The sweat and grime on the Woods Masters face illuminated through the light.

"Oh, you won't believe who he's hurt. Who he has watched die."

Oliver turned around, his pace increasing as he walked into nowhere.

"I'm not done Oliver."

Oliver faced The Woods Master, his expression grim. His fists were clenched.

"Trust me, Melanie," Oliver said, "Whatever the Woods Master tells you, he's manipulating it."

That's when Oliver sprinted; he ran into The Woods and the battle began again.

The Woods Master nodded at Walter and he clicked a button on his shirt. Suddenly, right next to where Melanie had been seconds ago, an explosion thrust up and out of the ground. A shard of glass hit Hazel in the shoulder and she screamed, hitting the floor. Cora rushed out to help her, dropping her sword. Chaos spiraled around Melanie. Natalie and Ashley were fighting the other villains and The Woods Master threw explosions dangerously close to Melanie's best friends. She heard a scream come from Cora and found that a dog had attacked her and left a giant scrape on her stomach. Blood was seeping through her shirt and Hazel was trying as fast as she could to mend the wound with her t-shirt (while still having a glass shard in her shoulder). Realization hit Melanie in the guts like she had been run over by a train. The Woods Master had brought back spirit dogs.

Around Melanie, trees were collapsing onto each other, smoke was rising from the hilltops and toxic fumes consumed her lungs. In the chaos, Melanie heard The Woods Master kneel down to Walter.

"Natalie, your wife…"

"I'll handle her myself. And her sister too."

He sheathed a small but extremely pointy dagger from his trouser pocket and pushed his way through the torment.

"STOP!" Melanie pushed herself to keep moving forward but realized she had too many things to do. She couldn't save everyone. She needed to pinpoint the source of the issue.

"HEY!" she called. The Woods Master looked down at her. "WHAT WAS THE THING YOU DIDN'T WANT ME TO KNOW ABOUT OLIVER?"

He sneered.

"Oliver knows a lot. Too much. He knows things that will happen today, tomorrow, in a decade that others don't want to happen. And could he do something about it?"

BOOM. Something happened and Merlin was on the floor.

"Who knows… But what I do know is he stays in a cave. He avoids the danger and does not risk anything to help the people he knows will perish."

"THAT'S NOT HIS FAULT. AND THE MORE HE INTERACTS WITH OTHERS THE HIGHER CHANCE HE HAS A VISION. HE JUST DOESN'T WANT TO ENDANGER PEOPLE MORE."

"Well," the Woods Master said, "What if he knew that one of your friends was going to die?"

There was an explosion. A tree fell down. Smoke covered Melanie's eyes.

Chapter 41
Lost Control

"Wha—"

The Woods Master's foot stomped on the floor and Melanie was sent flying. She crashed into a tree and almost knocked herself out.

"What? What? WHAT?!"

She had lost all comprehension of her situation.

She dropped her plan. Dropped her strategies.

What?

Melanie could only see red dots. She felt a ringing in her ears and the pounding of her heart slowly died down.

Cora and Hazel appeared next to her in an instant.

"Walter just injured Natalie!"

"He's holding Rhea!"

Melanie's brain stopped working. She shoved down everything: her thoughts, questions, panics and just barreled her way to Natalie and Rhea.

And there he was; standing over an injured Natalie and holding Rhea up to his weapon.

"Do. Not. Move." said Melanie.

"Natalie, you stand down and let us do our thing... then your sister doesn't get hurt.

Rhea's eyes fluttered open and she gasped at the site of Walter.

"Hello there, Realm Jumper. It's good to see you again."

"No!" said Natalie, grimacing as she stood up. She still held her wounded arm in her other hand.

"Well then," Walter took out his dagger.

"NO. STO—"

Rhea widened her eyes, snapped her fingers, and disappeared out of thin air.

"Oh my gosh," Hazel gasped, "She brought up enough energy to teleport."

Walter dropped his hand, livid.

"Fine," he growled, "If you guys are going to play dangerous, then I know who's next."

He dashed away back to the Woods Master.

"We need to get out of here," Natalie stated, "All of us."

"Bu—"

"She's right," said Cora, "I thought Natalie had evacuated Riverhaven but—"

"The Woods Master is planning to destroy it," Hazel

whispered.

"What do you mean?"

"Don't you see? All he ever wanted was to have it. But he can't. So he thinks that if he can't have it, no one can. The Woods Master is planning to kill Riverhaven and everyone and everything inside of it."

"And once he's done," Natalie gasped, "Once he's done using Walter's hatred for the place to destroy it, he'll dispose of Walter too."

Melanie cheeks flushed with terror.

"Oliver... We need Oliver," she said.

"He's not going to come," said Hazel and Cora at the same time.

"Not the bitterness..." Melanie cried, "Why are you guys always so bitter towards him? What did he do?" Hazel and Cora didn't even have time to meet Melanie's eyes because they all heard another loud explosion.

"Oh my god!"

They had spent so much time arguing that no one had noticed that Ashley and Merlin were missing. In front of them was the Woods Master and Walter, but not alone. They were circled by Spirit Dogs, the ones that are used to suck out all the energy of Riverhaven. But unlike last time, these dogs looked fiercer, scarier, more intent on eating a town. And there were also millions. They spread throughout the whole entirety of Melanie's eyesight. But it wasn't only that that terrified the crew.

In the Woods Master's hand, dangling from his palm, was Ashley, choking in his grasp.

"LET GO OF HER!" Rhea screamed, appearing in front of The Woods Master out of thin air.

"Help me! Help me! Help me!" Ashley thrashed around The Woods Master's palm like a three year old throwing a tantrum.

"Don't worry!" Hazel shouted.

"We'll get you down," added Cora.

"I have finally wrapped the town in my paint bullets. Everyone there is encased. There will be no survivors. And definitely no witnesses here!" The Woods Master beamed.

Walter snapped his fingers and suddenly a mountain of human beings and Riverhaven creatures fell on top of the crew.

"Riverhaven is going to die. But I want at least some of the townsfolk and creatures to witness it happen."

The Spirit Dogs planned to attack as many people as they could. Hazel and Cora stood their ground to fight them, Natalie and Rhea ran to attack Walter without actually hurting him. Meanwhile, Melanie was running to Merlin. She had seen him unconscious on the floor earlier in the battle and knew that he had all the answers and could help her right away.

***

"Merlin! Get up right now. Come on man. We really need you."

Melanie tried everything she could to shake him awake, but he wasn't giving in. Melanie didn't know what had happened to him, but he was already sick enough and shouldn't be in battle. Melanie needed to take him to somewhere quiet where she could get answers on how to stop The Woods Master and her dad. But more importantly, about what the Woods Master had meant when he said one of her friends was going to die.

Melanie used the remaining force in her arm to pick up Merlin. Surprisingly, he was very light and limp. That was worrying. Melanie turned around and saw that the Woods Master noticed her. She swallowed down saliva and soot and started to run away as fast as she could, holding Merlin. Within a second, explosions were firing at her from left to right.

Melanie's legs fired up in fear and vigorously stomped

on the ground, spraying dirt onto the soles of her feet. Merlin was pulling at the muscles in her arms (which were still bruised with glass and dirt and many other materials) and she pushed through the pain, straining out the remaining miracle energy in her. A bottle hit the floor and instantly blew up in her face. She choked, spitting out the ashes out of her mouth.

She ran.

And ran.

And ran.

And ran.

A spirit dog who she didn't notice had been following her tried to bite at her legs. She kept running, perturbation fueling the energy she knew it was impossible to have. The Spirit Dog growled and dug its teeth into Melanie's faded denim jacket. Melanie roared in agony as she threw off her jacket in an impromptu attempt. Her breathing returned to almost normal as she saw the Spirit Dog getting distracted by ripping her jacket to shreds. After a couple more agonizing and excruciating minutes of running with Merlin slung over her shoulder, the explosions ceased and the air cleared. She laid him down on the floor and bunched up her shoulders against the tree next to him.

She lightly slapped him on the head a couple times and

then his eyelids fluttered awake.

"So Merlin, tell me..."

***

Hazel could sense the chaos in her lungs, building up and ripping its way through each and everything. Cora had been helpfully wounding spirit dogs with Excalibur enough so they couldn't use powers to absorb Riverhaven. Natalie and Rhea had successfully managed to get a couple stabs at The Woods Master. He was still alive and Ashley was still dangling from his hand, but they still did something. The Tailless snake and the other villains were nowhere to be seen. Which means the only person Hazel could target was Walter.

And Hazel knew just how she was going to do that. She fumbled through her bag to find what she was looking for.

The day that she had met Melanie was also the day Merlin had given each one of the girls a very special gift. Hazel remembered so clearly how meaningful hers had felt.

"This locket will let you see into two people's hearts, literally. Put the golden heart above the person's heart and you will hear all of their thoughts and wishes. And if you really want to, you can grant one of them. You can grant anyone's wish. But beware, you can only use it twice."

Hazel had used it once on Cora so that they could escape one of the Woods Master's plans. She thought the locket was all just for fun. But Hazel had just realized that Merlin had intended her to use it for a different reason. All along Merlin had known what she needed to do. If it doesn't work, everyone will die.

Slowly, Hazel started to approach Walter.

"HAZEL!" Cora screamed to her in the distance, "What do you think you're doing?"

"Trust me," she said. Her lips quivered. Hazel had been scared to ask a clerk at the only store in the woods for a free bag with the cute designs on it. How was she going to do this?

Hazel noticed how, slowly, people were stopping their fights to watch her; until no noise could be heard in the forest except an occasional boom. All the townsfolk and creatures who had been summoned, watched quietly, some fixing their wounds.

"Hazel," Rhea whispered, "Stop."

But she didn't stop. Instead, she unlocked the locket from around her neck and held it firmly in her palm. She met Walter's eyes.

"Walter. Someone very brave named Melanie McGee taught me and everyone here that a Bond is a trait. It is something that can happen, you can do, etc. But it doesn't mean that it consumes you. That doesn't mean that because you have that Bond, your whole purpose is to complete it, carry it on. It is meant to be an attribute, not a prison. And I know that all you want is to be happy with your wife and child and live in a place where you get recognition for what you do. All along, you convinced yourself you wanted power because your Bond makes you destroy others for it. But in truth, everyone has felt that. I thought I couldn't fight in battles like how heroically Cora does because I can only see good in people. But it's helped me so much because now I can help you break free from this awful man."

Hazel directed everyone's attention to The Woods Master. He scoffed unconvincingly.

"Idiot girl. She's just making up lies, Walter. You came here to do something... DO IT."

Walter unsheathed his dagger again but his expression faltered.

"He's using you, you know." Cora stepped up, holding her hands in the air to symbolize she can't do any harm. "He's been using you since the day you told Melanie that you stole the feather."

Walter's eyebrows arched together in confusion.

"L-lies," he stammered, but his own words did not

match his expression.

"Come on, Walter," The Woods Master hissed impatiently. "DESTROY THEM."

Before anyone could make a second move, Hazel grabbed her locket and shoved it into Walter, straight in the chest. He lost his balance and fell to the floor. He sneered at her in disgust but Hazel knew that the gears had already started to shift in his brain.

Walter was sprawled on the floor. He looked unconscious but in truth the locket was just doing its job.

"Hazel!" Cora exclaimed, "You're a genius. That locket shows everyone their biggest wish and makes it come true."

"But his biggest wish is to not have the Bond he has," said The Woods Master, beaming, "And the locket can't do that. So your stupid plan won't work."

"Actually," said Cora, standing up straight, "Because the locket can't grant that gift, it can do what Walter always needed. The locket will make him realize that his Bond doesn't control him. And neither do you."

The Woods Master's jaw popped open.

"No. No!"

"You can continue denying yourself through the pain but it's not going to work this time," said Natalie.

Walter's eyes snapped open. He looked at Hazel and

the rest of the crew and smiled.

"Goodbye."

As the power of the locket shot him into the air, he took one last second to wink at Hazel.

She had never felt more heroic in her entire life. All the ideas of being weak, or dumb had faded away.

"You saved us," Cora gave Hazel a hug and smiled.

Walter McGee was back.

"UGH. NEVER MIND HIM," The Woods Master bellowed in utmost enrage, "I WILL DO IT MYSELF."

BOOOM! An explosion resounded through the forest.

***

BOOM! Melanie heard an explosion resound through the forest.

She hoped that her friends were ok.

"Melanie," Merlin smiled, "It's good to see you've got your wits back again."

Melanie smiled for a split second and then grasped Merlin's hand seriously. "We do not have a lot of time, Merlin. Oliver disappeared, of course during the moment we really needed him. But that's not the bad part. The Woods Master told me that Oliver had visions of people I know in danger."

"Yes," Merlin interrupted delicately, "He had that vision of you sprinting through the forest carrying me as you were encircled by fire. That, I'm guessing, just happened."

"Yes, yes, yes. Doesn't matter," Melanie continued, "The Woods Master told me Oliver has had a vision of my friend dying. Is that true? Was The Woods Master just trying to freak me out to get me distracted? Merlin this can't be true... Can it?"

Melanie was biting her lip.

Merlin looked down.

"Merlin, is it true?"

No response.

"Melanie, darling these aren't my questions to answer. But what you do need to know is that you need to find Oliver and get back to help everyone fast, soon."

"But Merlin—"

"I don't want to leave you hanging so I'll answer one of your questions. Hazel and Cora have history with me from way back. They both didn't have any parents and so I was their father figure. But Oliver has history with me too. He's my best friend and only I can understand him. I've mentored millions of young pupils over my years... When Hazel and Cora started to get to know him and learned he had visions, they were great friends. However, this one time, years back, Oliver had a vision that put the girls in a state of ultimate terror. They didn't believe it was true and they assured themselves and everyone that they would make sure it would never happen. But visions don't work like that, dear, no matter how bad you want to change it. They fought with Oliver for months. They begged him to make sure it would never come true. They told him that if he was a real friend, a real hero, he would find a solution. But he knew, I knew, that destiny is unchangeable."

"Merlin... What are you saying? What was his vision? Are you implying someone is actually going to die? Merlin, what's happening?"

"Get back to the fight. And no matter what you think, listen to Oliver."

"Merlin wait—"

He snapped his fingers and then he was gone.

***

Melanie found herself back in the battle scene.

"Melanie!" Cora jogged up to her. "You're back.

Yeah, is what she tried to say, but instead she just choked herself up.

Melanie noticed something was off. The Woods Master looked stiffer and more agitated as he tried to attack both Ashley (in his hand), Rhea and Natalie at the same time with his giant feet. People looked more hopeful.

"Where's my dad?" she asked.

Cora smiled wide.

"I'll give you a run through..."

While Cora updated her on the news, Natalie had broken off from fighting The Woods Master to encourage the mythical creatures and townsfolk to fight as much as they could, use the weapons they could make, and put in all their force into taking the Woods Master down.

"Oh yes! That's awesome!" exclaimed Melanie tearfully, upon the end of hearing the story.

Cora hugged her wholeheartedly.

Melanie turned around to see Oliver straight in her face. She jumped back, surprised. Then she scowled.

"Come with me."

He grabbed her wrist and brought her to the center of the battlefield where the townsfolk and creatures were attacking The Woods Master's villains, and where The Woods Master himself was still torturing Ashley.

"What? Why am I here? What do I need to do?"

Oliver fell flat on his face and started to snore.

"What?" Melanie rolled her eyes annoyed, "Oliver, what the heck. Get up right now. We're in the middle of the biggest fight of the universe."

"He's having a vision." Merlin magically popped up behind her.

"What? Right now?"

Melanie heard Hazel scream as an explosion had just grazed her hip area. She heard a townsfolk say:

"Someone help Cora Perkins. She's a main fighter and there's a gash on her forehead."

Ashley was struggling and Rhea was weak. Melanie needed to help.

But before she would do anything, Oliver grabbed her by the hand. His whole complexion was droopy and dull. He grabbed her ear and whispered something.

"No. Way," Melanie said stubbornly.

"Melanie..." Oliver whispered, aggravated, "This was my vision. You need to do it now."

"Your visions are dangerous," Melanie hissed back.

"And no matter what you think, listen to Oliver."

Melanie groaned as she remembered what Merlin had said.

So in the turmoil of disarray, Melanie pointed her index finger and tapped the shiny golden bracelet on her wrist three times.

The first noise Melanie heard was a howl. Then a roar, a flutter of wings.

Everyone dropped their weapons.

"Woah," said Natalie, her mouth wide open.

It was a miracle.

It was stunning.

What were exactly 55,000 mythical creatures straight from the pit of Riverhaven had flown into the battle scene. The day she Melanie had met Merlin came running back to her memory.

"Made entirely of pure gold, this bracelet, if you tap it three times, something magical will come to the rescue. But, like many powerful magical elements, it can only be used once. You'll know when the time comes."

The magical thing Merlin had given her was every single creature that ever inhabited Riverhaven. They were going to save it.

The Woods Master dropped Ashley and she fell into Rhea's arms.

The animals began to swarm everything until all that Melanie and everyone else could see was the radiance of the creature's powers. Melanie looked at Merlin and grinned in delight. He winked back.

Hazel, Cora, and the rest of the townsfolk stared at Melanie in awe.

The moment was interrupted by a bomb that had blown up right in Melanie's peripheral vision. Once again, she and her friends were knocked into trees. The Woods Master stomped his way up to them.

"This...ends ... now"

He picked up Merlin by the neck and squeezed him in rage until his veins could be seen popping out from his grime covered fingers. Merlin groaned weakly as the Woods Master squeezed the life out of his eyes.

A single, pearly tear streaked down Oliver's cheek.

Hazel and Cora began to cry.

"Guys," Melanie gasped, worried, "Merlin is immortal. No matter what the Woods Master does..."

The silence tore up Melanie's insides. Merlin lay in the palm of The Woods Master's hand, his breathing gone.

Merlin was choked by The Woods Master's strong grip.

"Guys..." Melanie started to panic, her eyes tearing up. "What is going on?"

Fire started to blaze onto people's clothing, spreading

up the tree they were against.

Townsfolk in the background were shouting as they tried to escape the smoke. The creatures Melanie summoned had killed off most of the spirit dogs and scared away The Woods Master's minions but Melanie was more concerned with something else.

"Guys! I know we can't reach Merlin but he's immortal... Why is everyone acting like Merlin is going to die?"

Melanie felt like she had been run over by a train. "No..."

More fire surrounded the crew.

Melanie's knees buckled, the hot heavy tears streaming down her puffy cheeks.

Merlin's skin was starch white and his limp body collapsed in The Woods Master's grip. All of his minions and all of Riverhaven's creatures had stopped moving, all staring at The Woods Master as he slowly killed Merlin.

Melanie sobbed and sobbed looking up at the Woods Master murdering one of her best friends, helpless. She looked at Oliver, his dull, emotionless eyes flooding with tears. Cora let out a dry sob and fell to the ground, heartbroken. Merlin was dying.

The Woods Master gripped his sword and pointed the

tip at Merlin's neck, laughing as the light left his eyes.

Chapter 42
A Riverhaven Miracle

All of a sudden The Woods Master paused. His eyebrows furrowed in confusion and he bent over in agony as if he had felt a sharp pain to his side. He dropped Merlin as he gasped in pain. Merlin landed beside a tree and Cora and Hazel rushed to feel his pulse. Slowly, his limp body became erect and Melanie cried in relief as Merlin sat up, looked at her with his silvery-blue starry eyes and smiled.

"You can't get rid of me that easily,"said Merlin, his eyes twinkling.

The group burst into cheers all giving him hugs and kisses. "I thought you were going to leave us," whispered Oliver through the tears.

The moment was interrupted by the sound of The Woods Master wailing in pain. That's when the 55,000 Riverhaven animals that Melanie had summoned began to encircle the Woods Master and strings of silver dust began to pull from his skin. They were physically stripping him from his power!

The Woods Master withered, quite literally. He

screamed in despair, like the force of his roar would keep him alive. Unicorns. Griffins. Monerines. Dragons. Elves. Goblins. They were all swarming the man, barely even harming him. Their physical force wasn't the thing killing him. Melanie was sprawled on the floor, gasping for breath. Hazel and Cora looked delirious as The Tailless snake shriveled to the floor. Somewhere in Melanie's peripheral vision was the blurry image of Natalie and Rhea, sighing in relief as King Henry and the goblin fell to the floor as well.

Melanie realized that for the first time in years, all the mythical creatures of Riverhaven were fighting with mortals. That's what killed Melanie's enemics. That was what was killing the Woods Master. Because the only power that he could use to win was creating chaos. He only had power when he could manipulate everyone to be against each other. And now his nightmare was a reality. Because the energy and dominance of Riverhaven being fully united was picking the pieces off of the Woods Master. He dropped out of the air and onto the floor with a hard THUD. Miserably, he cried as the torment of power embraced him. Embodied him. The soul of Riverhaven ripped the man apart.

He grasped Melanie's hand as his last attempt of arrogance. He grabbed her ear and whispered. A scratchy voice rasped against her ear. He struggled to keep his body up as he whispered his last words. Melanie could feel them echoing through her skull.

And then the world went silent.

Chapter 43
End

Melanie's burned skin tingled as she looked around in exhaustion. Fires were still blazing around her, spirit dogs layed on the first floors of the Thicket, slowly dissipating into dark brown ashes. It was deadly silent; only the crackles of the fires and the echoes of destruction could be heard, yet everything seemed so sinister. Hazel and Cora were still sprawled on the ground, their fragile eyes not fully understanding what they were living through.

The large gash on Melanie's arm was begging for attention and the new cut on her lip and heat exhausted feet (without shoes) were bleeding and not helping Melanie with her search for Oliver and Merlin. Her squinting eyes looked around but she couldn't find their bodies anywhere on the unpaved floor. Still hung in the air was the Woods Master, his body lifeless and his once giant corpse and hand that he had used to grab Ashley, lay still in the air, his chin laid back as if he was basking in the dark and harsh glare of the clouds and dust obscuring the rays of the sun that had been there an hour ago. He looked so at peace, even though he was dead.

Wow, dead. Melanie felt delirious but the anger in her still blazed quietly. How could so many people get hurt, so many houses burned, so many lives affected, and she was only ten minutes late to save everyone? Some small child was sobbing in the background, dust painted on his face.

Somewhere in the air, was Melanie's father, free from the curse he thought he was born with. But Melanie knew he wasn't coming down from his dragon just yet. There were people in Riverhaven who needed an explanation. Melanie didn't expect it to be a short one. A tree behind her caught on fire, and the fiery smoke bled into her eyes as she coughed forcefully, trying to turn her head away and ignore the pain in her neck. Natalie, with her splintered hand was tying up all the minions of the Woods Master. Rhea laid unconscious, her navy robes smoldering. She wore shredded and tarnished fabric instead of clothes now.

Melanie let herself cry, still semi conscious, as she watched the fires and debris from the explosions. Riverhaven was broken. Who knows how long it will take to heal.

Epilogue

Melanie's dream of being a fairytale character had come to life, her lifelong desire accomplished, though facing obstacles she would never have imagined. Melanie sat down on the large leather armchair of her favorite bookstore.

"Wow. Can you believe that this was actually real life?" said a spunky teenage girl, exiting one of the aisles, a sword at her waist and carrying a book with a long gold spine.

"I know, right Cora?!" exclaimed the strawberry blonde who had her phone up, on Facetime with a bearded man who resembled a younger-ish Santa Claus. "Hopefully you will be able to join us all, Merlin! After your hospital stay. Then we can go back into the town of Riverhaven."

"Oh, come on, guys!" said Natalie, handing a book over to her husband. "Let's try to get some well-deserved rest before we start thinking about our next traumatic adventure."

Hazel, Cora, Natalie, and Walter all laughed.

Melanie smiled from her chair, capturing the happy moment.

"Hey, where's Oliver?"

"Right here!"

The once scrawny boy emerged 1 foot taller, looking

just like a 45 year old man again.

"Guys! Look! We're famous!"

He snatched eight copies of a leather-bound book and passed them to the cashier. He handed her a 100 dollar bill and put the books in a bag.

He took one out and laid it on the desk. It had a shiny cover, with images of dragons, a singular unicorn, trolls, and a snake without a tail. Three young girls were at the front, along with a young mom and a bald-ish dad.

Slowly, Oliver opened the cover. Swirls of ink filled the first page. In big, bold golden letters was

The Tale of Riverhaven

On the last page, there was an image of seven people, looking back at their own fairytale.

"Melanie, what did The Woods Master actually whisper in your ear before he died?" asked Hazel. Melanie smiled wistfully.

"He told me: Don't let your Bond control you."

Natalie's eyes widened in recognition.

"Wait... but...that...that means that—"

"I know," said Melanie.

The Tale of Riverhaven's pages all came to a close. The book fell shut as The Woods Master's final words stayed etched on the page.

About the Author

Sienna Rapaport is currently thirteen-years-old but wrote The Tale of Riverhaven as her first published book when she was only eleven. She was very inspired by her teachers to start writing and has had short stories published in many newsletters and magazines, such as Stone Soup. The Tale of Riverhaven has been being developed for almost three years and she is so excited to finally get to publish it. She is very grateful for her friends and family to continue to push her and always support her.